THE CRUEL COUNT

It was certainly not the reception Lady Vesta Cressinton-Font had expected.

As soon as she left her ship and set foot on the small Mediterranean island of Katōna, the blue-eyed, exquisitely-beautiful Vesta felt frightened and totally alone. Where, she wondered, were Prince Alexander's representatives? Surely His Royal Highness would not let his future bride arrive on Katōna without a formal greeting. Really, it was quite unthinkable: traveling all the way from England to marry a man she had never met and then being rudely abandoned . . .

"They tell me you have arrived alone."

The words cut across Vesta's indignant reverie. Startled, she directed her gaze toward the man who spoke them. His stern, domineering manner, his penetrating glance quite alarmed her. And yet he was so darkly handsome . . .

"I am Count Miklōs Czakó," the stranger continued harshly. "I will take you to His Royal Highness."

Bantam Books by Barbara Cartland
Ask your bookseller for the books you have missed

1 THE DARING DECEPTION
2 NO DARKNESS FOR LOVE
3 THE LITTLE ADVENTURE
4 LESSONS IN LOVE
5 JOURNEY TO PARADISE
6 THE BORED BRIDEGROOM
7 THE PENNILESS PEER
8 THE DANGEROUS DANDY
9 THE RUTHLESS RAKE
10 THE WICKED MARQUIS
11 THE CASTLE OF FEAR
12 THE GLITTERING LIGHTS
13 A SWORD TO THE HEART
14 THE KARMA OF LOVE
15 THE MAGNIFICENT MARRIAGE
16 BEWITCHED
17 THE IMPETUOUS DUCHESS
18 THE FRIGHTENED BRIDE
19 THE SHADOW OF SIN
20 THE FLAME IS LOVE
21 THE TEARS OF LOVE
22 A VERY NAUGHTY ANGEL
23 CALL OF THE HEART
24 THE DEVIL IN LOVE
25 AS EAGLES FLY
26 LOVE IS INNOCENT
27 SAY YES, SAMANTHA
28 THE CRUEL COUNT
29 THE MASK OF LOVE

BARBARA CARTLAND
The Cruel Count

THE CRUEL COUNT
A Bantam Book

PRINTING HISTORY
First published 1974 by Pan Books Ltd.
Bantam edition / December 1975

Bantam Books are published by Bantam Books, Inc. Its trade-
mark, consisting of the words "Bantam Books" and the por-
trayal of a bantam, is registered in the United States Patent
Office and in other countries. Marca Registrada. Bantam
Books, Inc., 666 Fifth Avenue, New York, New York 10019.

PRINTED IN THE UNITED STATES OF AMERICA

Chapter One

1819

Vesta stepped onto the jetty and felt the earth still heaving beneath her. Then she walked further down the Quay and stood looking round.

She had expected Katōna to be beautiful, but not as breath-takingly lovely as it was.

The small harbour with its wooden houses and red-tiled roofs was picturesque enough, but beyond them were the dark-green of the olive groves and again beyond them the mountains luxuriantly wooded, until silhouetted against the blue sky were the dazzlingly snowy peaks of a mountain range.

Everywhere there were flowers.

Flowers in the window-boxes of the little houses, flowers on the lower slopes of the mountains, in the ravines, under the olive trees, patches of brilliant colour which left her breathless at the wonder of them.

"My new country," she whispered to herself.

Her blue eyes were shining in her small heart-shaped face as she waited for a man in the uniform of a Petty Officer to walk across the Quay towards her.

He saluted smartly as he said:

"I have paid ten men who will carry your baggage to the Inn, M'Lady. Would you allow me to accompany you?"

"No indeed, Mr. Barnes," Vesta answered. "I know the Captain is having difficulty in holding the ship in this heavy sea. He will wish you to return as swiftly as possible."

"But M'Lady, there should be someone to meet you."

"I anticipate that they will be waiting at the Inn," Vesta replied. "After all they could not be sure of the exact time or indeed the exact day of our arrival."

"Indeed no, M'Lady, and they can count themselves fortunate we are here at all."

The Petty Officer smiled as he spoke and Vesta smiled back at him.

"It was rather a frightening voyage at times," she said, "but I have arrived safely and I am deeply grateful. Will you please convey my thanks to the crew?"

"I will indeed, M'Lady, it has been a privilege and an honour to have you aboard."

"Thank you, Mr. Barnes."

Vesta held out her hand. He shook it and said:

"I would like on behalf of myself, M'Lady, and every member of the crew, to wish you great happiness in the future."

"Thank you, Mr. Barnes," Vesta said again.

He saluted before walking smartly back along the jetty to where the boat was waiting which had carried the Lady Vesta Cressington-Font and her baggage from the ship.

It was manned by eight British sailors and Vesta repressed an impulse to wave to them, thinking it would seem too over-familiar.

Instead she turned and walked slowly after the men who were carrying her trunks upon their backs. Some of them were so old, she noticed with a feeling of consternation, and they were almost bent double by their burden.

It was strange, Vesta thought, that the elegant, gossamer-fine gowns that constituted her trousseau should weigh so much.

But she was not particularly interested in her trunks at the moment, but rather in the people she saw standing outside their houses and working around the harbour, knowing that with them lay her future.

The men were dark-haired and sturdily built with strongly defined features, the women were plump, full-bosomed and undoubtedly attractive.

They had smiling faces and their skin burnt by the hot sun was a golden brown.

The children with bright inquisitive black eyes wore little red caps on their heads with long tassels, which were a part of their national costume.

"It is a lovely country with nice people!" Vesta told herself.

She remembered when her father had first mentioned Katōna she had looked at him in surprise.

"Katōna?" she had queried.

"Do you know where it is?" the Duke of Salfont had enquired.

Vesta hesitated a moment.

"In the Mediterranean?" she had queried and had then given a little cry. "But how foolish of me! Of course I know! It lies between Albania and Greece and is independent of the Ottoman Empire ruled over by the Turks."

"That is right," the Duke approved. "I am glad you are so well-read."

"I must confess to have very little knowledge about the country," Vesta admitted. "But I think I am right in saying that they were not affected by the war."

"You are right," the Duke replied. "Napoleon Bonaparte did not conquer Katōna, so they have escaped the devastation which affected so much of Europe, nor have they sacrificed their menfolk."

There was a bitterness in his voice which Vesta did not miss. Any reference to the war would bring back to him all too agonisingly the fact that he had lost his only son at Waterloo.

Vesta realised that ahead of her the baggage-porters were entering the courtyard of a small Inn. She followed them and a man who was obviously the Inn-Keeper appeared in the doorway bowing low as soon as she had reached him.

This was the moment she knew that she had to show how proficient she was in the language she had been studying so arduously during the long voyage from England.

"You were expecting me?" she asked gently, hoping he would understand.

"Yes! Yes! Gracious lady."

"There are people here to meet me?"

He shook his head and burst into a long explanation of which she understood barely one word in ten.

What was clear was that there was no-one there!

But it seemed they had expected her, the Inn-Keeper had also believed that a number of personages would have arrived in time to welcome here.

Still talking the Inn-Keeper led Vesta along a narrow passage into what she realised was a small private parlour. It was a pleasant room.

It had paned windows looking out on one side onto the Quay, on the other onto a small garden bright with flowers, in which she saw her first orange tree bearing the golden fruit.

When Vesta had been shown the parlour a large stout woman of middle age, obviously the Inn-Keeper's wife, curtseying respectfully offered to take her upstairs.

Vesta entered a bed-chamber where she understood she could wash or change her clothes should she desire to do so.

But as she had just come from the ship, she merely put the heavy cape she had worn in the boat down on the bed and went down the narrow wooden stairs again to the parlour.

Going to the window she could see outside in the harbour the schooner which had brought her from England riding uneasily at anchor. A boat was being taken aboard and Vesta felt suddenly afraid, seeing her last link with England leaving her.

In the ship there were fifty men who knew her, who spoke her language, who were her countrymen, and they were now leaving her alone in a strange country which had not even bothered to send a representative to greet her on arrival.

She could not understand it!

The Prime Minister, His Excellency János Sutez, had been explicit in telling her exactly what to expect.

"His Royal Highness will not meet you at the Port," he had said, "He will wait for you at the Palace in Djilas. But you will be received by Baron Milovan, a very distinguished noblemen who has a magnificent Castle half way between Jēno where you will disembark and Djilas where you will be received with every possible ceremony."

"Who else will be with the Baron?" Vesta had enquired, feeling she must be prepared for everything.

The Prime Minister had understood her anxiety. He had explained in detail matters of lineage, and even the personalities of those who would constitute her first contact with her new country.

There would be two ladies besides the Baron's wife. There would be a number of Courtiers, Statesmen and Noblemen to be her escort to the capital.

"The first day will be quite informal," the Prime Minister had said. "They will expect you to be a little tired after your long journey, and you will drive to the Baron's Castle where you will stay the night.

"The following day it will only take you two hours to reach Djilas, but you will have luncheon at another fine mansion outside the city, belonging in this instance to a distinguished member of the Prince's Government."

He smiled.

"There you will be able to change into your very best gown with which to dazzle the people who will undoubtedly be lining the streets to cheer you when you enter the city."

"And the Prince?" Vesta had asked.

"His Royal Highness will be waiting for you on the steps of the Palace. He will know of course the exact moment of your arrival and as the carriages draw up he will come half way down the steps to meet you."

He smiled.

"Were I able to be there I would have had the honour of presenting you, but in my absence it will be the Baron who will perform that little ceremony."

Vesta had drawn in a deep breath. That moment she knew would be the most frightening of her whole journey.

She moved across the small parlour. What could have happened? How was it possible there was no-one here?

The Prime Minister had made it very clear that she

was expected to disembark at Jēno. There was a larger port further down the coast, but Jēno was nearer to the capital.

In fact it was only five hours' drive, but it had been planned that she should break her journey at the Baron's Castle.

"They must have mistaken the day of my arrival," Vesta told herself.

But she knew that the Prime Minister had said they would definitely reach Jēno between the 25th of May and the 1st of June.

Today was only the 26th, so she was not late! And supposing she had arrived the day before, would they have expected her to wait alone in this small Inn?

She partially answered the question by remembering that they would certainly not have expected her to be alone!

But even so, she could imagine how infuriated the Prime Minister would have been had he accompanied her and found himself treated in such an offhand manner.

The Inn-Keeper came bustling into the room and Vesta understood that he was asking her if she would like something to eat.

"Thank you," she replied, "I would like it very much."

It was only about noon, but she did in fact feel quite hungry.

The ship had managed to take on new supplies at Naples, but she found that after such a long voyage she was heartily tired of the few dishes at which the cook was proficient, and had found herself eating less and less every day.

A table was laid for her in the window looking into the garden, and a moment or two later a young girl with golden skin and two long plaits of jet black hair came into the room carrying a large dish.

It smelt delicious, and having seated herself at the table Vesta discovered she was eating a fresh fish covered with the egg, oil and lemon sauce which the Aide-de-camp to the Prime Minister had described to her in glowing terms.

He had also been her teacher not only with regard to the language which she had studied with the Prime Minister, but about the customs of the country, the food, the entertainments and the amusements of its people.

"As you know," the Aide-de-camp had said, "our people are a mixture of Greeks, Hungarians and Albanians—the Hungarians being predominant socially. We therefore have acquired the tastes and characteristics of all three countries."

He smiled.

"Where food is concerned perhaps the Greeks have made more impact than the others! As we have a long coast-line our seafood is good, and even when the women fail in other aspects of cuisine, they still produce excellent fish dishes!"

There was no doubt that the fish which Vesta was eating now was very good.

To follow it there was lamb, young and tender, cooked on a long skewer with tomatoes and a green vegetable she did not recognize but which tasted rather like green peppers.

The lamb was garnished with herbs and she told herself that once she had arrived at the Capital, she must learn more about the vegetation of the country.

She had found in fact that the Aide-de-camp and the Prime Minister were unable to answer half the questions that she posed to them.

The Inn-Keeper brought her a light white wine to drink and, while she had also asked for some water, she sipped the wine and found that it was very pleasant.

She wanted to ask if it was grown locally, but that was beyond her vocabulary.

In fact not only did she find the Inn-Keeper hard to understand, because he had a very different accent from that of the Prime Minister and the Aide-de-camp, but it was clear that except for a few words he also found her almost incomprehensible.

When Vesta had finished luncheon she realised it must be nearly one o'clock and she guessed that the inhabitants of the little Port would soon settle down to a siesta.

Looking through the window she could see a number of old men were sitting on chairs or on their doorsteps with nodding heads and closing their eyes against the brilliant sunshine.

"What am I to do," she asked herself, "if no-one ever comes for me?"

It was a frightening thought. Supposing they had forgotten all about her? Supposing she just sat here day after day, month after month? Supposing she ran out of money and could not even pay for her food.

She might have to work for her living! What could she do? Work in the Olive Groves, help in the Inn?

She gave herself a little shake. This was the sort of day-dreaming for which her mother had scolded her very often.

"You are too imaginative, Vesta," she used to say. "You have got to learn to be more practical, more down-to-earth! It is no use living in a fairy-tale world!"

It was, Vesta had told herself severely, her most regrettable fault, and yet she found it hard to cure herself of what at times could be a magical experience.

She remembered two or three years ago hearing her father and mother discussing her when they did not realise she could overhear what they were saying.

"I am worried about Vesta," the Duchess had said.

"Why?" the Duke enquired.

"She is so introspective. She is not the least like the other girls. She lives in some fanciful world of her own and half the time is unaware of what is going on around her."

"Perhaps that is a good thing," the Duke smiled.

"It is nothing of the sort!" the Duchess snapped. "Vesta expects too much of people. She always thinks they will live up to her own ideals."

"Then she will be disappointed," the Duke predicted.

"She will be hurt and unhappy," the Duchess said, "because when one expects so much there are always deep disappointments."

She sighed.

"Vesta is too sensitive, too introspective, too imaginative."

"She will grow out of it," the Duke said firmly.

But Vesta knew she had not grown out of it. If anything, her imagination had increased as she grew older.

But she had promised herself before she left England that she would be very circumspect, very sensible, and not surprised by anything however different, however unaccountable it might seem.

"I must not expect too much of anyone," she had said and knew that what she really meant was of one person in particular.

She walked across the room feeling restless and again a little afraid. Should she go for a walk by the Quay or should she just wait hoping someone would arrive?

Because she felt so restless she forced herself to sit down in an arm-chair.

There was no fire in the big grate which in the winter could hold a huge log of wood. There was something rather empty and comfortless about it now, and Vesta felt her spirits sinking lower and lower.

It was then she heard voices outside in the passage. There was a loud voice speaking authoritatively and beyond doubt in a cultured manner.

She could not understand what was being said but she thought that here at last the welcoming party had arrived. Instinctively she stiffened a little, sitting more upright in her chair.

The Duchess had said to her as she left:

"Remember to be dignified, Vesta. You have every reason to be proud of your breeding and your father's importance. And you are English. Hold your head high, and remember, whatever happens, not to show emotion."

"I will try, Mama," Vesta said meekly.

Now she hoped her face was expressionless as the door was flung open and a man strode into the room.

Despite her resolution Vesta could not help feeling surprised at his appearance.

He had thick black hair, broad shoulders but a narrow-hipped, thin and wiry figure. She thought she had never seen a man with such an arresting face!

His features were sharp cut with a high-bridged nose between two hard penetrating dark eyes which stared at her so searchingly that she felt embarrassed.

'His manner is impertinent!' she thought.

She noted with astonishment that his clothes were covered in dust, the polish of his boots almost obscured by it, and instead of a cravat round his neck, his shirt was open showing the sunburnt skin of his neck and chest.

"They tell me you have arrived alone!" he said and his voice seemed to echo round the room. "Where is the Prime Minister?"

There was something imperative in the way he spoke and Vesta sat up a little more stiffly.

For the first time since she had arrived at Katōna, she felt angry. She had felt alarmed before at not being met, but the manner in which this stranger had burst upon her and was now addressing her aroused her resentment.

"As, Sir, you are apparently aware of my identity," she said slowly, choosing her words with care, "it would perhaps be courteous if you would introduce yourself before asking me questions."

The Gentleman stared at her for a moment as if he was surprised at her reply. Then he shut the door behind him and advanced further into the small room.

He seemed very over-powering and as his almost black eyes met Vesta's blue ones, she thought to herself:

"He looks like an eagle!"

"My name," the stranger said, "is Czakó—Count Miklōs Czakó—and I have a message of great importance for the Prime Minister."

His English was excellent; there was only a faint accent, little more than an intonation, to show it was not his native tongue.

"Then I am afraid you will have to go some distance to give it to His Excellency," Vesta answered.

"What the Devil do you mean by that?" the Count snapped.

Then seeing the shocked surprise on her face he added quickly:

"Your pardon, My Lady! I should not have spoken in such a manner! But I have instructions for His Excellency from the Prince."

"You have come here from His Royal Highness?" Vesta inquired.

"Yes."

The reply could not have been briefer.

"I imagine that there must have been some mistake, or perhaps a muddle about the date of my arrival," Vesta said slowly. "His Excellency, the Prime Minister was expecting Baron Milovan to be here to greet me."

"Where is the Prime Minister?" the Count asked again.

She knew by the tone of his voice that he had found the fact she had not answered his first question extremely irritating.

"His Excellency is in hospital in Naples."

"In hospital!"

"We had a very rough voyage through the Bay of Biscay," Vesta replied, "but it was nothing to the storm we encountered on entering the Mediterranean. Indeed the Captain thought at one moment the ship might founder."

"And the Prime Minister was hurt?"

"He broke a leg. It was a bad break and the doctors in Naples at the hospital to which we took him declared it was quite impossible for him to travel for at least another two weeks. It was His Excellency himself who insisted that I should continue my voyage."

"Alone?" the Count enquired. "Where are the rest of the people who should be with you?"

Vesta could not help two dimples appearing at either side of her mouth as she smiled. She was well aware that the Gentleman in front of her was confused and bewildered by what she had to impart, and because he had upset her it amused her to disconcert him.

"After we left Naples," she said, "when in fact we were looking forward to arriving at Jēno, a number of the ship's crew were taken ill. This happened on the twelfth day after sailing, and ever since everyone on board has been coming out one by one in spots that

were so profuse and so ugly that we feared at first that
they had contracted smallpox."

"Smallpox!" the Count ejaculated.

"Fortunately our fears were groundless," Vesta went
on. "It was in fact a very unpleasant and virulent form
of chicken-pox."

"But surely your attendants . . ."

"The lady who chaperoned me and the Aide-de-
camp both succumbed yesterday," Vesta explained,
"and this morning they are both running high tempera-
tures. The Aide-de-camp's was in fact over 103°. It was
impossible for them to come ashore."

"Good God!"

There was no doubt that the gentleman in the dusty
riding clothes was shocked at the information Vesta
conveyed to him.

He stood for a moment looking down at her, at her
blue eyes twinkling a little because his astonishment
amused her, at her very fair hair silhouetted against the
darkness of the arm chair.

Then he said harshly:

"As the Prime Minister is not here, I must therefore
explain to you what has happened. The reason you have
not been welcomed to Katōna, Lady Vesta, is that a
Revolution is taking place!"

"A Revolution!"

It was Vesta's turn to be surprised.

The Count nodded.

"It began about a week ago, and the Prince has
therefore decided that it would be best for you to return home. That is the message I was to convey to the
Prime Minister."

Vesta was silent for a moment. Then in a voice she
hardly recognised as her own she said:

"Are you seriously . . . suggesting that I should go
. . . back to England?"

"It would be best."

"After I have come all . . . this way? It has been a
. . . long and difficult . . . journey."

"I am aware of that," the Count said, "but a Revolution can be dangerous and one is not yet certain of the
outcome."

"You mean the Prince might be . . . deposed or forced to . . . abdicate?"

"There is always that possibility."

"But it has not happened . . . yet?"

"No, not yet."

Again Vesta was silent for a moment and then she said:

"And how do you suggest that I should return? My ship has gone. It is now sailing to Athens, from which it is anticipated that both my chaperone and the Aide-de-camp will be well enough to return to Katōna either by ship or overland."

"There must be other ships," the Count said quickly.

He looked out of the window as he spoke, as if expecting to see one in the harbour.

"Even if there were one," Vesta said calmly, "I would not board it. I have no intention of returning to England."

"That is a ridiculous attitude!" the Count said sharply. "You know little about this country. I imagine you know little about Revolutions, you have never had one in England. You must think of yourself and leave for safety."

"I have chosen to come here," Vesta replied, "and whatever happens I consider it my duty to stay."

"Good God, woman, it is not for you to make the decision!"

The Count spoke so violently and Vesta rose slowly from her chair. She stood facing him and now her eyes were flashing blue fire.

"I cannot imagine that because there is a Revolution," she said, "the officials surrounding His Royal Highness must lose all sense of propriety. You will please apologise for speaking to me like that."

Their eyes met and for a moment Vesta thought the Count intended to defy her. Then he said quietly:

"I apologise, and I hope that you will forgive me. It is only that I am deeply concerned for your safety."

"I prefer to decide such things for myself," Vesta answered. "And now will you answer one question: Is His Royal Highness in danger?"

The Count appeared to be considering before he replied:

"I cannot answer that with any certainty. He may be."

"In that case," Vesta replied, "I should be at his side."

"It is impossible!" the Count retorted. "I have His Royal Highness's authority to beg you to return home. When things are more settled in Katōna, an emissary can journey to England and discuss the matter of your marriage further."

He paused before he continued.

"At the moment it is in your best interest to go back. I must find a ship to carry you."

"I have already told you, Count," Vesta said patiently as if speaking to a backward child, "that I have no intention of leaving Katōna. There is no point in any further argument. I must ask you and . . . if necessary . . . command you . . . to take me to my . . . husband."

For a moment the Count was absolutely still.

Then he said, and there was no mistaking the stark astonishment in his voice:

"Your—husband?"

"The Prince and I were married by proxy before I left England," Vesta replied. "The Prime Minister has the papers with him."

"Married! But—the Prince was not aware of this! It is the Prime Minister's doing! The wily old fox!"

"I understood," Vesta said, "that His Excellency was carrying out the wishes of His Royal Highness in asking for my hand. But it was in fact my father who insisted on the marriage before I left. He did not wish me to travel on a basis of 'sale or return'. "

Then as the Count seemed too stupified to speak she added ironically:

"How right he was! Although he would not have anticipated that I would have been asked to leave almost before I had arrived!"

The Count scowling ferociously walked across the room to the window overlooking the Quayside.

"If this is true," he said after a moment, "it can of

course be rectified. A marriage by proxy is only a legal ceremony. As the Prince is head of the law in Katōna, the marriage can be declared invalid."

Vesta drew a deep breath.

"That is something, I think, which should be discussed only by the Prince and myself, and not by outsiders."

Her voice was very cold and the Count turned from the window to say:

"Very well, Ma'am, I am of course obliged to obey your command. I will take you to His Royal Highness. But let me say this. If at any time during our journey to Djilas you change your mind, I shall be very willing to bring you back here, or to find you a ship at some other port which will convey you in safety to England."

"I am most grateful for your consideration," Vesta said with a touch of sarcasm in her voice. "Kindly tell me when you wish us to leave?"

Her voice brought a different expression to the Count's face.

"Immediately!" he replied. "I should explain that the reason I posted here with such haste is that your life may be in danger. There are certain people who do not—wish you to stay in Katōna."

Vesta stared at him uncertainly.

"You mean they intend to assassinate me?" she asked.

"They might have merely forced you to return on the ship on which you arrived," the Count answered. "But as that has left I would not give much for your chance of survival."

"Those are the ... Revolutionaries, I ... suppose?" Vesta questioned.

He nodded.

"Does that make you see sense?" he asked. "Go back to England, Lady Vesta. Return to a country where there are no Revolutions, where you are known and loved. Go back to the people you understand. Go back to your family, to security, to comfort and peace."

He was almost pleading with her now.

"You are very persuasive," Vesta replied, "but may I remind you that as I am married to your reigning

Prince I imagine I have some authority in this country.
I therefore . . . command you to take me with all possible speed to His Royal Highness."

She had spoken quietly but her eyes were still bright
with anger.

The Count looked down at her and she knew he too
was incensed. He obviously had not expected that she
would defy him.

There was no doubt, she thought, he was like an eagle—cruel, a bird of prey, imperious, ruthless.

She wondered for a moment with a little tremor of
fear if in fact he was not really a messenger from the
Prince, as he had claimed to be, but a member of the
Revolutionary bands who were stirring up trouble.

Then she told herself she had no choice but to trust
him. Quite unexpectedly he capitulated.

"Very well, Ma'am, I will obey you," he said. "But
do not blame me for the consequences, whatever they
may be."

"I will not," Vesta replied.

"Then change quickly," he said. "You had better tell
me which trunk out of that mountain of baggage you
wish taken upstairs."

"We shall be riding, I suppose?" Vesta asked.

"We shall be riding," he answered, "and you can
take nothing with you, except what can go in the saddle-bag and that had better not involve much extra
weight. What you had best remember is to take a warm
cloak—it can be cold at night."

Vesta wasted no more time. She turned towards the
door and when he opened it for her she went outside
into the passage.

Her baggage almost filled the small entrance to the
Inn. Fortunately the Duchess had insisted that Vesta
should acquaint herself with every item in each individual trunk.

The Count was standing beside her impatiently and
she had a moment of panic when she could not remember where her summer riding-habit was packed.

Then she pointed to a round-topped leather trunk,
and the Inn-Keeper and the young girl who had waited
on her at luncheon carried it upstairs.

In the small low-ceilinged bed-chamber Vesta put her hands up to her cheeks. It had been hard to battle with the Count, but she could not help thinking now that she had come much better out of the contest than she might have expected.

There was something inflexible and over-powering about him, and she knew that he had been determined that she should return to England. She had felt him willing her to go, she had felt that he almost pushed her physically from his country, as if he disliked the very thought of her being in it.

'I hate him!' she told herself, 'I hate him!'

It was not often that she felt so strong an emotion about anyone, in fact she had never before been so disturbed by a man.

Then she told herself it was because the Count was a foreigner. Foreigners were much more positive in their feelings and in their manner of speech than the English.

Even so, he had no right to have spoken to her as he did. No right to have been so rude, to have sworn in her presence, or have attempted to force her into a decision she did not wish to make.

"I hate him!" she whispered again, and yet she had to trust herself to him.

There was no-one else, no-one to whom she could turn for help or guidance, and if the Count was right she had enemies who wished to destroy her.

It was a terrifying thought, and yet Vesta told herself she was certain the Count was making the most of the situation, perhaps exaggerating the fact that there were people who did not wish her to marry the Prince.

Nevertheless, Vesta told herself sensibly, there must be some truth in what he had to say.

After all there was no denying the fact there had been no-one to meet her on arrival, and the Count must have ridden hard and furiously with the Prince's message for the Prime Minister.

When she thought of him, she realised that never before had she seen a gentleman, except her brother, without a cravat round his neck. And never before had a gentleman spoken to her in the manner the Count had done!

The young maid having opened the top of her trunk was waiting her instructions. To Vesta's relief her summer riding-habit was easy to find.

She quickly divested herself of the pretty muslin gown she had put on to come ashore. But when she looked at the green silk habit she knew it was far more suitable for a trot round Rotten Row than for what was likely to be a hard ride to Djilas.

However she had nothing else to wear, and there was some consolation in knowing that the full silk skirt and the white braided jacket with big pearl buttons became her. It also accentuated the smallness of her waist.

There were several blouses to wear with the habit, and because it was so hot Vesta chose one of white muslin inset with lace. Then she sent the maid downstairs for a hatbox.

"Be careful of your skin," the Duchess had said before Vesta left. "Remember the sun will be much stronger than in England! And as undoubtedly your pink and white looks will be attractive to the darker skinned Katōnians, it is important you should not get sunburnt."

She had looked at her daughter's almost ethereal loveliness and added as if afraid she might grow conceited—

"Anyway a lady should always have a white skin."

From the hat-box Vesta took out a wide-brimmed straw hat trimmed with green silk leaves to match her riding-habit and ribbons of the same colour to tie under her small chin.

In 1819 the new tight waist and fuller skirts had been introduced to London from Paris. Corsets were back for those who needed them, but much more becoming were the petticoats that were once again in vogue. Underneath Vesta's riding-habit she wore two stiff white petticoats edged with lace.

There were white gloves to match the braid on her jacket and a small gold-handled riding-whip which had been a wedding present from one of her sisters.

She could not help feeling pleased with her appearance. There was however the problem of what else she should take with her. She was quite aware that the Count might be disagreeable if she took too much and she was determined not to give him cause to find fault.

So she merely wrapped a brush, comb, toothbrush and some spare handkerchiefs in one of the diaphanous nightgowns which were part of her trousseau and covered them with a piece of paper.

The few cosmetics she needed, and they were very few, she slipped into the pocket of her jacket.

Then picking up the heavy black cloak she had thrown down on the bed on her arrival, she went downstairs.

The Count was in the parlour and she realised that he had taken the opportunity in her absence to tidy himself.

His coat had been brushed, his boots rubbed with a cloth, and what Vesta thought was a decided improvement, he was wearing a cravat!

By no means a conventional neckcloth, it was little more than a silk handkerchief wound round his neck and tied in a knot, which would have aroused the contempt of any English Dandy. But at least it covered the nakedness of his neck.

As Vesta entered the parlour the Count had a glass of wine in his hand and there was an empty plate on the table to show he had ordered something to eat.

He rose to his feet.

"Surprisingly quick for a woman!" he remarked mockingly. Then as he met her eyes he added, "Ma'am."

"You appeared to think it important we should leave immediately, Count," Vesta answered, "I would not wish to involve you in any danger."

She saw his lips twist in a faint smile before she added:

"I should be grateful if you would arrange for my luggage to be put in a safe place. When I reach Djilas I imagine I can send for it."

"But naturally," the Count replied, "if the Revolution is over."

"I had of course taken that fact into consideration," Vesta replied coldly.

"I have ordered the horses," the Count remarked. "They should be outside."

Vesta had ridden ever since she was tiny, and no horse was likely to prove too much for her to handle. But she did not expect the small rough-coated animals which stood waiting outside the Inn.

They were quiet, sturdy and by no means the spirited horse-flesh to which she was used or what she had expected.

The Count saw the expression on her face and laughed.

"They are the right type of beasts for where we are going, Ma'am," he said, "though undoubtedly not what might be expected to complement your Ladyship's attire."

He was jeering at her, she thought, and she hated him with an intensity which frightened herself.

He took her cloak from her and laying it across the horse's back tied it firmly to the saddle. The small parcel of her clothes he put in the saddle-bag slung on his own horse.

The Inn-Keeper was standing in the doorway. Vesta held out her hand.

"Thank you," she said in Katōnian, "for looking after me. I am very grateful for all you have done, and please keep my baggage safely."

It was difficult to find the right words, but the Inn-Keeper understood. All smiles he promised to guard her luggage with his life. He thanked her for her condescension and wished both her and the Count 'God speed' on their journey.

The man in charge of the horses helped Vesta into the saddle, the Count had already mounted. As they rode away over the cobbled roadway he said:

"So you have taken the trouble to learn our language!"

"I know a little, and it would be a pity for my endeavours to be wasted," Vesta replied.

"But naturally, Ma'am," he answered.

Again there was a mocking tone in his voice which made her sure he was laughing at her.

Once they had passed the houses and the cobbles ended, the road became dusty and now Vesta could see the olive groves and the profusion of flowers which she had sighted from the Quay.

Never had she imagined there could be so many colours bordering the road and climbing up the hillside in a panorama of beauty.

There were red poppies, pinks, marigolds gold, purple and white and clovers which she recognised as well as cyclamen, yellow iris and wild gladioli besides the vivid dazzling blue gentians.

There were also a great number of other flowers of which she did not know the name. But she did not feel like asking the Count what they were because she had the feeling that he might find her curiosity amusing.

They had however only gone a very little way on the road before moving ahead of her he took a pathway rising up the hillside.

Vesta followed him so intent on looking at the beauty all around her that she was not particularly interested in which direction they took.

Now there were numbers of orange trees and she thought how thrilled her sisters and their children would be when she could write home and tell them she had actually seen oranges growing among their green leaves.

There were lemons too and a fruit that she imagined was a pomegranate, but was not quite certain.

It was after they had been riding for nearly half an hour that Vesta was aware that they were climbing all the time.

Now when she looked back she could see the little port lying far away behind and below them, its red roofs clustered closely together, while ahead were only mountains and more mountains rising higher and higher towards the snowy peaks.

In a little while the flowers too were left behind. Now the path they were following twisted through tree trunks and yet climbed all the time. It was far cooler

and the sun coming through the green branches was
very beautiful.

There was juniper, copper, beech, myrtle and sometimes the purple glory of the Judas tree before they too
were left behind and replaced by oaks, firs and pines.

It was as they moved on steadily but surely, that
Vesta understood the Count's good sense in the choice
of the horses they were riding.

These animals were, she knew, used to the mountains, there was something in the way they moved, the
manner in which they did not hurry themselves and yet
covered a great deal of ground which told her that although they might not look spectacular, they had
tremendous endurance and were used to mountainous
regions.

The path through the trees was narrow and the
Count continued to ride ahead.

Occasionally he looked back to see how Vesta was
faring. He did not speak to her and she guessed that he
was still angry with her for ignoring his advice and insisting on him leading her to the Prince.

'Did he really mean, the marriage could be declared
invalid?' she wondered. 'But why having asked her to
come to Katōna to be his wife should the Prince wish
to be rid of her?'

Then Vesta realised she knew the answer to that
question. It was something which lay at the back of her
mind like a menacing shadow.

Something she had tried not to remember and yet
she knew now she was forced to face the truth.

Chapter Two

Everything that had happened to Vesta had been so unexpected. Even now she still felt breathless at the manner in which it had occurred.

She had been planning this Spring to enjoy her second Season in London. Her first season the previous year had been a success, as was to be expected when a débutante so important as the daughter of the Duke and Duchess of Salfont was introduced to the *Beau Monde*.

But Vesta was, as it happened, already well accustomed to the social round.

The Duchess of Salfont had been entertaining for her five older daughters one after the other ever since anyone could remember. And somehow it had been inevitable that Vesta should take part in the festivities even though officially she was still in the schoolroom.

She had, therefore, since she was fifteen been invited to parties with her sisters because many of the Duchess's friends, struck by her beauty, felt she enhanced any social occasion which she attended.

A number of young men had even asked the Duke if they might pay their addresses to her, only to be dismissed summarily with the words—"she is much too young".

Then in February a month after her eighteenth birthday there had come a bombshell in the shape of the Prime Minister from Katōna.

Vesta could recall vividly her astonishment when her father had called her into the library of Salfont House in Berkeley Square and had said to her in a tone that was unusually serious:

"Vesta, I wish to speak to you."

She had wondered uneasily what was coming. She knew of old that those particular words usually prefaced a complaint or a scolding. But instead the Duke said:

"I have received today a visit from His Excellency the Prime Minister of Katōna. He informed me that His Royal Highness Prince Alexander of Katōna requests the honour of your hand in marriage."

As Vesta stared at her father too astonished to speak, the Duke added:

"It means that, since Katōna is an independent Royal Principality, you will in fact be virtually Queen of that small but important country."

For a moment Vesta could not believe she had heard her father correctly. Then she said almost childishly:

"But I do not . . . know the Prince."

Her father had taken her hand in his and drawn her down beside him on a sofa.

"My dear, where Royalty is concerned marriages are arranged, and I cannot help thinking that the Prince's advisers have been very wise in suggesting an English bride for their Ruler."

"You mean," Vesta said slowly, "it is the suggestion of his . . . Government not . . . His Royal Highness . . . that I should be his wife."

"As I have said," the Duke replied, "these things are arranged for the best diplomatic and political reasons. I have in fact, Vesta, already consulted the Foreign Secretary Lord Castlereagh, who is extremely anxious that we should acquiesce in Katōna's wishes in this matter."

"But, Papa, I have never seen the Prince!" Vesta cried.

"I believe he is a well behaved, charming young man," the Duke answered, "who has as it happens, English blood in his veins; for his grandmother and his great-grandmother were both English."

He paused before he went on:

"Katōna has always been friendly with Great Britain and it is very important she should remain so."

The next day the Foreign Secretary, Viscount Castlereagh, made the same point as Vesta sat with him and the Prime Minister, the Earl of Liverpool in the Drawing-room at 10 Downing Street.

It was rather awe-inspiring, but at the same time Vesta had liked Lord Castlereagh. Tall and dignified having inherited much of his mother's beauty, his physical and moral courage had made him outstanding among Foreign Secretaries.

But because he was the idol of many women he knew better than the Prime Minister or the Duke of Salfont how to handle a sensitive girl.

"I see that I must tell you my secrets," he said quietly. "Katōna is extremely important in our re-construction of Europe. Since the Conference of Aix-la-Chapelle last year and the readmission of France to the Concert of Europe, we are desperately trying to maintain the balance of power."

Vesta had always taken an interest in politics and she understood what he meant.

He smiled at her beguilingly as he continued:

"At the moment I am firmly resisting the plans of Alexander, the Tzar of Russia, together with Prince Metternich, the Austrian Chancellor, to institute a league of European powers and to guarantee the existing order under the sanction of military force."

"I am sure that would be a mistake," Vesta exclaimed.

"I can see you have a grasp of these matters," Lord Castlereagh said, "and that is why you can understand that we are most anxious for you to go to Katōna and use your influence with Prince Alexander."

He saw the expression on her face and said:

"I know the Prince, Lady Vesta, and I promise you he is intelligent and a good sportsman."

'Will he love me?' Vesta longed to say, but knew that was a question no-one expected her to ask.

The Prime Minister, handsome despite the fact that the cares of office had stamped their mark on his face, was as persuasive as the Foreign Secretary.

"I can assure you, Lady Vesta, that there is no-one we would rather see as the wife of the Ruler of Katōna than your father's daughter."

He smiled at her.

"I am well aware from my long acquaintance with your family how much this country means to you all and that no-one—and I mean that in all sincerity— could be a better Ambassador for Britain."

'High-sounding words!' Vesta had thought when she returned home.

But they still left her with the prospect of marrying a man she had not even seen and of whom she knew nothing except that Statesmen spoke well of him.

As if he sensed the tumult within her, Lord Castle-reagh's last words were meant to be consoling.

"I have visited Katōna, Lady Vesta," he said. "The scenery is very beautiful and the flowers are a delight both to the eye and the mind. Sometimes nature can give us what people fail to do!"

Now that she had come to Katōna, Vesta knew what he meant.

At the same time not even the Foreign Secretary of England had anticipated that she would arrive in the middle of a Revolution to find herself unwanted.

Then as she thought about the Count's insistence that she should return home, she realised with her knowledge of diplomacy that the Prince would not compel her to return even though the Revolutionaries might have done so.

For him to take an action of that sort would un-doubtedly cause a diplomatic incident between Great Britain and Katōna. Their engagement had been widely publicised in the newspapers and even mentioned in Parliament.

Although Vesta had had little time to get together a trousseau and to sail on the date that was expected of her, a large number of parties had been given in her honour.

The wedding presents had numbered hundreds, in-cluding one from the Prince Regent—a Chinese bowl of great antiquity which had aroused the admiration of all who had seen it.

"No," Vesta told herself, "the Prince will not dare to force me to return however much he might wish to do so."

She decided too that the Count had definitely over-stepped his orders in trying to bully her into leaving the country.

Then the thought which had over-shadowed her arrival returned to her mind to jeer at her.

Because her day-dreams and romances were so much part of her life, she had tried to tell herself a fairy story about herself and Prince Alexander.

She had believed, with a childish faith, that when they met they would fall in love with each other.

After all, even Mama told her that Katōnians being dark admired fair women, and Vesta would have been extremely stupid had she not known that she was very pretty.

It was not only the young men she met at parties who told her so. She had recognised the expression of admiration on the face of almost everyone she met.

For her own taste she was too small and too slight, compared with the statuesque beauty of her sister Angelina, and too simple in comparison with the sophisticated Charlotte.

But there was no doubt that her skin was very white, almost translucent, compared with the other girls. Her vivid blue eyes were larger and more expressive than those of the usual blonde beauties while her hair in the sunshine looked like spun gold.

At times Vesta could be very critical about herself, but at other times she visualised herself to be a Princess in a fairy story, journeying across the world to meet Prince Charming. When they met she was sure they would live happily ever after.

She began to imagine the things they would do together when they were not on duty.

She learnt from the Aide-de-camp that the Prince was an exceptionally good horse-rider, perhaps because his mother was Hungarian.

"The Hungarians are magnificent horsemen, are they not?" Vesta asked.

"There are no words to describe them," the Aide-

de-camp had answered enthusiastically. "They seem
part of their horses and they can make their animals
perform incredible feats."

This had become an intrinsic part of Vesta's dreams.

'We will ride together over the countryside,' she pre-
tended. 'He will also drive me in his Phaeton and we
will watch his horses racing as I have watched Papa's.'

She had imaginary conversations with her future
husband, telling him things that she had never told
other people because being married they would be so
close to each other.

Her day-dreams grew so vivid that at times she felt
that the Prince was more intimate to her than anyone
else had ever been.

She could visualise almost everything about him except his face. That remained a blank ready to be filled
at the moment they met.

Then almost like a physical blow, and far more dam-
aging, came the awakening.

They had entered the Mediterranean just before the
storm which was to throw the ship about as if it were
little more than a piece of driftwood and nearly cause it
to founder.

Because she longed for some fresh air, Vesta
wrapped in her thick cloak had gone up on deck short-
ly before lunch.

There was a strong wind and the sailors were taking
reefs in the sails and hurrying around with a purposeful
air which told her they were anticipating trouble.

The waves were already breaking over the stern in
shower after shower of spray.

By the time Vesta had been on deck for no more
than a few minutes, her cloak was wet and she had decided it would be more sensible to go below.

She had come down the companionway into the narrow passage which led to the large comfortable Saloon
where they sat and ate.

Just outside it there was on the wall a row of hooks
for the gentlemen to hang their oilskins, so they should
not make the luxuriously upholstered seats in the
Saloon wet or be forced to take them into their cabins.

Vesta undid her cloak, pushing back the hood from

her fair hair and then unbuttoning the large bone buttons one by one. There were quite a number of them and as she unfastened them she overheard the Aide-de-camp say:

"She is too young, too innocent, too unsophisticated to be able to cope with what lies ahead, you must realise that."

He spoke with a note of passion in his voice which was almost moving.

"I think that Lady Vesta has a lot of good sense," the Prime Minister replied in his deep voice.

Vesta stiffened. She realised that the door of the Saloon was ajar. Then she heard the Captain say:

"I agree with Your Excellency. I think her not only one of the most charming young women I have ever met, but she definitely has a great deal of character."

Vesta realised that it was because the Captain was present that they were speaking English. And she would have been inhuman if she had not wished to listen to what they were saying about her.

"But she is imaginative," the Aide-de-camp remarked, "she is also sensitive. How can she possibly deal with a woman like Madame Züleyha?"

"Has His Royal Highness not agreed to give her up?" the Captain asked. "When I was last in Katōna, the manner in which the people spoke of her, the hatred they showed for her, would have made any ordinary person flee the country in terror."

"They will not hurt her while she has the Prince's protection," the Prime Minister said dryly, "but I agree with you, Captain, and you do not know half of what I know: she is bad, her influence is appalling and she has done more to damage my country than it is possible to estimate."

"But you persuaded His Royal Highness to take a wife," the Captain said.

"I persuaded him without much difficulty because he knows that he must marry sooner or later," the Prime Minister replied.

"But when he does so he must give up this creature!" the Aide-de-camp cried. "This Turkish woman who has indeed confirmed that the Turks are, and always will be our hated enemies!"

Again the Aide-de-camp's voice was passionate and Vesta knew it was because he was enamoured with her.

She would not have been feminine if she had not realised that every day he was falling more in love.

Every day he found new excuses to be beside her, to teach her, to talk with her, and yet, because he knew his place, he would never presume to express his feelings.

"I asked you," the Captain said, "whether His Royal Highness has agreed to give up Madame Züleyha?"

"He implied that he would do so," the Prime Minister answered, but hesitatingly.

The Captain and the Prime Minister were old friends, who had known each other ever since they were boys. But neither the Captain nor the Aide-de-camp had any idea that a marriage by proxy had already taken place between Vesta and the Prince.

That had been kept a close secret. The only people who knew of it outside Vesta's immediate family were the Foreign Secretary, Lord Castlereagh, and the Earl of Liverpool.

Vesta was not surprised when the Aide-de-camp said in a voice which revealed all too clearly his inner feelings:

"If I had my own way I would turn this ship round and take Her Ladyship back to England! Can you imagine the shock it will be when she learns about Madame Züleyha, when she realises that the man she is already idealising and making into a hero, is besotted by a mistress who is loathed and despised by every decent citizen in our country."

Quite suddenly Vesta had realised she could not bear to hear any more. She had crept past the Saloon and gone to her own cabin to lie face downwards on the bed.

It could not be true! She must have imagined what she had overheard!

Just like a pack of cards, the castle she had been building in her thoughts collapsed around her, and then because it had been such a shock, because she could not bear to think of what she had learnt inadvertently, she had tried to forget it.

She had attempted to force it from her mind, to tell herself that when she arrived everything would be well, as she had dreamt it would be.

Yet despite herself, Madame Züleyha, whoever she might be, was now always present with every thought she had of the Prince.

"An evil woman" the Prime Minister had called her.

'And am I strong enough,' Vesta asked herself pathetically, 'to combat evil?'

She was so deep in her thoughts as they rode on through the woods, the sunshine making strange patterns of gold on the path ahead, that it was with a jerk she came back to reality and realised that the Count had drawn his horse to a standstill just ahead of her.

Her own animal trotted up to his side and he said:

"We have now been riding well over three hours and I think it is wise to give the horses a short rest. What is more, we have now come to a difficult part of our route."

"A rest would be very nice," Vesta answered.

She saw him dismount and realised that he would in politeness come to her assistance.

Because she had no wish for him to touch her, she lifted her leg over the pommel and slipped quickly to the ground.

The Count drew the horses off the path and seeing some grass under the trees they went towards it eagerly. Then he said:

"Walk a little way with me, I have something to show you."

She obeyed him, realising as she did so that the trees were thinning a little until abruptly they came to an end.

In the brilliant sunshine which almost hurt Vesta's eyes after the shade of the trees, she saw that immediately ahead of them was a great expanse of bare rocks devoid of any vegetation.

Stark and barren they rose high on one side of them, and on the other side fell sharply down into the distant valley.

For a moment Vesta was so surprised that she could

only stare, thinking that an avalanche or some natural catastrophe must have caused such devastation.

Then she realised that it was the glacier formation of past centuries, perhaps aggravated by the snows of the winter, but nevertheless there was nothing new or modern about it.

Staring at the sunlit stones she saw at the same level on which she stood with the Count, a small narrow path just wide enough for a horse to traverse!

It was a precarious path, stony and rough, and on one side of it a sheer cliff plunged hundreds of feet downwards to end in a profusion of rocks far down in the valley.

"Is that . . . where we . . . go?"

Even to herself her voice sounded weak and fearful.

"If you wish to continue on your journey to Djilas," the Count replied.

There was something in his tone which told her that he had brought her here deliberately to frighten her. He was not to know, she thought wildly, that she was terrified of heights, that she had always been petrified by them.

When she was quite small, her sisters had taken her up onto the roof of Salfont Castle, and being much older than she was they had climbed round the turrets and over the battlements and forgotten her.

An hour later they had found her rigid with fright, unable to move forward or backwards staring with wide eyes at the sheer drop just in front of her.

Nothing they could say could persuade her to move. She just sat there white-faced and trembling until finally they had fetched her brother, who had carried her in his arms to safety.

It had been a family joke after that, that Vesta would "never rise very high in the world!" But however much they teased her, Vesta's fears were very real.

Sometimes she dreamt that she was standing on a roof and sometimes in her dreams she fell and awoke with a scream.

She was aware that the Count was watching her face.

"It is now, if you wish to return, that it would be wise to do so. Once we have passed over the bare rocks and reached the woods on the other side it would be almost too late to go back."

His voice became persuasive.

"If we return now you can sleep in Jēno. Tomorrow I am quite certain we will find a ship which if it cannot take you to England will carry you to Athens where undoubtedly you could join up with the schooner which brought you here."

Vesta did not answer for a moment. She was looking at the narrow path over the rocks.

How could she face it? How could she possibly ride along it with a deep cliff almost inviting her to fall? The horses were presumably sure-footed, but even so they could make a mistake!

"It would be so much easier to go back," the Count continued. "I told you it was a difficult journey. But at the moment it is the only route safe from the Revolutionaries."

He put out his arm and pointed to the valley below.

"Look, there is the roadway we should have taken, or rather the one you would have travelled on in comfort and with much state to Baron Milovan's Castle."

Forcing herself with an effort to look down, Vesta followed the direction of his finger and saw far, far away between the mountains rising on either side of it, a twisting road winding its way beside a silver river until it disappeared into the distance.

It appeared empty and she wondered if in fact there were Revolutionaries forming ambushes on either side of it or advancing towards Jēno to prevent her entering the country.

Was the whole thing a figment of the Count's imagination, and was it really necessary for her to endure the dangers of this mountain path?

At that moment she would willingly have encountered a thousand Revolutionaries rather than journey along the cliff's edge.

"Go back."

She felt as if the Count had sensed her fear and was deliberately tempting her.

With an almost superhuman effort she managed to answer him proudly:

"I have already told you, Count, that I wish to reach Djilas," she said, "I see no reason to change my mind."

She turned away as she spoke knowing she could not bear to look any longer at the barren rocks.

Walking back into the shelter of the trees, she sat down beneath the great oaks to watch the horses cropping the grass.

The Count did not follow her and she wondered if he was too annoyed at having failed once again to shake her determination.

She sat looking into the wood. In the distance she saw a small roe-deer moving between the tree trunks, and she tried to divert her mind from what lay ahead, by recalling the animals that the Aide-de-camp had told her were indigenous to Katōna.

The jackal, porcupine, wild cat, the brown bear, the lynx were, she remembered, some of them.

"Of course there are eagles," the Aide-de-camp had said, "some of them very large. As the shepherds will tell you they are dangerous to the young lambs in the Spring."

"The Count is dangerous!" Vesta told herself, "he is trying to make me afraid. He is deliberately using every possible means to force me to leave the country."

Something strong and proud made her determined that she would not give in to him, and what was more she would not let him see how afraid she was.

But even so, when they re-mounted their horses and he went ahead onto the narrow rock path, she felt so frightened that she thought she must cry out and beg him to take her back.

'I must not . . . look down! I must not . . . look down,' she told herself.

And because her horse needed no guidance, following faithfully behind the one ridden by the Count, she shut her eyes and began to pray.

'Please God . . . do not let me be a . . . coward! Please God . . . do not let me . . . fall! Please God . . . keep me safe and . . . brave!'

Her eyes opened for a moment and she realised they had not progressed far. The cliff's edge appeared to be only a few inches from her horse's feet.

She shut her eyes again and went on praying.

Once her animal stumbled. She drew in her breath so sharply, it was like a knife in her breast.

"Are you all right?" the Count asked looking back over his shoulder.

His voice echoed round the barren rocks:

"All right—all right." Like a ghost it came back to her.

She could not reply. It was impossible to force any words to her lips. She could not even whisper her prayers, she could only say them in her heart.

'Please . . . God, no not . . . let me . . . fall!'

It seemed to her as if a century of time passed. The horses plodded on, their hooves ringing out on the loose stones, the jingle of their bridles seeming unnaturally loud.

Vesta had given up all pretence of doing anything but keep in the saddle. She was holding on to the pommel with both hands, her eyes closed.

She was so tense that she could hardly breathe, and then when she felt as if her fear encompassed her to the point of suffocation, she heard the Count say:

"Well, here are the trees again."

He spoke lightly, and hardly daring to believe him Vesta half opened her eyes.

It was true. They were out of the sunshine and into the shadow of the trees all around her.

It was then as she drew in her breath she knew she was going to faint. She gripped the pommel so tightly that beneath her gloves her knuckles must have shown white.

'How he will despise me,' she thought. 'How contemptuous he will be if he is aware how afraid I have been.'

With an effort and in a voice which even to herself seemed far away, she asked:

"Could we . . . stop for a . . . moment?"

"But of course," he said courteously.

She slipped from her horse's back without waiting to see whether he dismounted and walked away into the trees, moving steadily over the mossy ground until she thought she was out of his sight.

She was shivering with cold and yet there were beads of sweat on her forehead.

'I . . . must put my . . . head . . . down,' she told herself, 'I must put . . . my . . . head . . . down.'

When she was sure that he could not see her, she dropped on her knees and tried to bend her head. She fell forward half unconscious and her forehead struck the ground!

The shock of it forced away to some extent the suffocating waves of darkness. For a moment she just lay there. Then with an effort she rolled over onto her back and tried to breathe deeply.

Without realising she had done so she had taken off her hat as she had walked away from the Count through the wood. It had been an instinctive gesture to try and get air.

Now she could not even remember what had happened since she had dismounted from her horse.

'Breathe . . . deeply,' she told herself, 'in out . . . in out.'

The darkness was receding but she was still shivering and her fingers felt numb.

'How contemptible it is,' she told herself, 'to be such a coward!'

Why could she not be like other people, like her sisters, who had never been afraid to climb anything?

And then as she lay there fighting for breath, she heard the sound of footsteps and knew the Count was coming through the wood in search of her.

With an agonising effort she managed to sit up. Her head was swimming.

It was difficult to focus her eyes but she stared ahead of her, not turning round as he reached her side.

"You are all right?" he asked and for the first time there was some concern in his voice.

"Of . . . course," she answered forcing the words between her lips.

He took one look at her white face and drew a flask from his pocket. He took off the top which constituted a small cup and filled it.

"Drink this," he said.

She would have argued had it not been almost impossible to speak. Instead obediently she put out one hand, realised it was shaking and steadied it with the other.

She took the little cup from him and put it to her lips. The brandy seared her throat, but even at the first sip she felt better.

"Drink it all," the Count said commandingly.

She obeyed him because it was easier to obey than to argue with him.

She could feel the spirit moving through her body like fire. Now her fingers were no longer numb and her hands were not trembling.

She could feel him towering above her and thought he must be gloating over her weakness.

"I am ... ashamed to ... say," she managed to articulate at last, "that I felt a little ... sea sick ... or should it be ... land-sick? My Uncle who is an ... Admiral has always ... told me that it takes him ... forty-eight hours after he ... has been at ... sea a long time to get his ... balance."

The sentence was really a triumph. Every word was difficult to enunciate but she managed it.

"Of course it is quite understandable," the Count said in a deep voice. "I believe many people feel uncomfortable after a sea voyage, just as Lord Nelson used to be sea sick when he returned to his ship after leave ashore."

Vesta handed the Count back the silver cup.

"I am all ... right ... now," she said, "and of course ... you will want to ... continue the ... journey."

She wondered how she would get to her feet, but he bent down and helped her.

For once she was grateful that he should touch her and did not hate him for doing so.

He picked up her hat.

"You have bruised your forehead," he said unexpectedly.

"I ... I ... walked into a ... branch ... of a ... tree," Vesta said quickly.

"It must have had sand on it," he remarked dryly.

Then keeping his hand under her elbow he helped

her back through the wood to where the horses were patiently waiting for them.

He picked her up in his arms and lifted her into the saddle.

"Do you feel well enough to go on?" he asked. "We have not far to go to the Inn where we must stay the night."

"I am . . . quite all . . . right," Vesta replied proudly.

"Do you wish to put on your hat?" he asked.

She realised he had carried it in his other hand and she had been too bemused to think of it.

"No, I do not . . . need it," she answered.

"Then I will take it with me," he said.

"Not if . . . it is any . . . trouble."

"It is no trouble," he replied. "Tell me if you wish to stop again."

"Your . . . your brandy has cured my . . . sickness," Vesta said. "I am sure I shall be . . . all right . . . now."

She did not dare look at him in case he should see through her pretence. She could not bear him to know that it was only her cowardice and her fear of heights which had made her feel so faint.

'How he would despise me,' she thought.

But sea-sickness was something no-one, however important they were, could prevent.

They set off again. Now the sun was low in the sky and the thickness of the trees made the wood seem dark and mysterious.

'I wonder if there are dragons somewhere in the patches of green darkness,' Vesta thought.

When she was a child she had always imagined that dragons lived in fir-woods and had told herself stories about how she was rescued from them by Knights in shining armour.

But no-one, she thought, would have imagined the Count was a Knight in shining armour. Rather he was like the Devil himself trying to tempt her into shirking her duty and, when she would not be tempted, evoking all the fires of hell to support his vendetta against her.

'The fires of hell,' she told herself, 'are the right simile, for I would rather encounter them any day than the ride again along that cliff's edge!"

Chapter Three

Their path now was straight and the woods were dense on each side. Then quite unexpectedly the trees cleared and Vesta saw ahead of them a building.

It was not a very prepossessing sight, for the building was rough half-timbered and its roof was held down with large stones.

It appeared at first sight to be derelict: most of the windows had no glass in them and some were blocked with what appeared to be rags.

Her expression must have shown her surprise, for the Count explained:

'It is an Inn used only by woodcutters and an occasional hunter after bear or chamois. It is the only possible place to rest, and I cannot believe you will relish riding through the night toward Djilas."

"No of course not," Vesta said, "and at least it will be a roof over our heads."

She tried to smile as she spoke, but they had now drawn nearer to the Inn and at close quarters it looked even more dilapidated than it had at first. What was more, she had the suspicion that it was extremely dirty.

The Count dismounted and because Vesta was staring at the building she was not quick enough to reach the ground before he lifted her from the saddle.

"There will be stabling of a sort where I can put these animals," he said.

"I will come with you," Vesta said quickly.

She felt reluctant to enter the Inn alone and perhaps have to explain her presence.

The Count had been right in supposing there would

be "stabling of a sort." There were just two rough byres, into which he put the horses and removed the saddles.

There was water in a bucket in each byre and some rather mildewy-looking hay, which however the animals began to chew with apparent relish.

"They are used to roughing it," the Count said with a smile as he secured the byres by a wooden bar which was attached with a piece of rope. "But what about you?"

"I dare say I shall manage as you will," Vesta replied coldly.

She felt he was hoping that she would be uncomfortable. She moved ahead of him with her head high and told herself that however rough the Inn might be she would not complain.

They walked through the low door into a room which held a large fireplace in which a big log was smouldering.

There were two large wooden settles on either side of the fire and a table at the other side of the room with four rickety wooden chairs. There were no other furnishings of any sort.

A middle-aged woman appeared wearing native dress. She was dirty and untidy and very unlike the smiling attractive women Vesta had seen in Jēno.

Her apron was badly in need of a wash, her dress was stained under the arms and her dark hair was straggling down her back.

The Count greeted her, and she replied in a dialect that Vesta found impossible to understand.

It appeared that the Count was familiar with it, because after a long exchange of words between them he said to Vesta with what she thought was a mocking glint in his eye:

"Bad news, I am afraid. The woman says her husband is out hunting for meat and is not likely to return tonight. There is in fact nothing to eat in the house."

"Nothing?" Vesta asked and realised as she spoke that, if not excessively hungry, she was certainly ready for a meal.

"The woman says there is nothing," the Count repeated. "She keeps hens and she will kill and cook one for us to carry away tomorrow. But that will certainly take time."

"If she has hens," Vesta suggested, "then she should have eggs."

"That is of course an idea."

The Count turned to the woman and Vesta knew by the way she nodded her head that she agreed there were eggs.

"Listen, do not offend her," Vesta said to the Count, "but ask her if she would mind if I cook the eggs. Explain to her that I have just come off a long voyage at sea and my stomach is very weak. I would not like to hurt her feelings, but I am sure I can cook better than she can."

"Would it matter if her feelings were hurt?" the Count asked.

"Of course it would!" Vesta said sharply. "Tell her what I have said."

The Count obeyed her and the woman shrugged her shoulders as if it was a matter of indifference to her who did the cooking.

She walked through a doorway which Vesta was sure led to the kitchen. She had been right when she supposed it would be dirty.

There was grease on all the tables, the place smelt, and the pots and pans hanging over the fire-place burnt black were indescribably filthy.

Picking up a basket the woman passed on through a door which led outside the Inn, and Vesta knew she had gone in search of eggs.

A moment later there was a loud squawking and clucking from a hen, and she guessed that the Inn-Keeper's wife was catching it to kill for their meal tomorrow.

She looked round the kitchen wondering where to start, and then finding a pan she followed the woman outside.

There was no sign of her and Vesta thought she must have gone into the wood after the hen who was reluctant to be slaughtered.

But as she had expected, only a little way from the

Inn there was a small cascade of water coming down from the side of the mountain and running between the trees.

This was obviously where the Inn-Keeper procured his water, but Vesta realised that, while she could lift a bucket onto the stones under the cascade, once it was full it would be too heavy for her to move.

She went back to the front room where she discovered the Count taking logs from a big pile in the corner and putting them onto the fire.

"I am afraid I need some help with a water-bucket," she said.

If she had not disliked him so much she would have been amused at the expression on his face.

"A bucket?" he questioned.

"I have to clean a pan before I can use it."

He stared at her for a moment, then he smiled.

She realised it was the first time she had seen him smile in genuine amusement, and it suddenly transformed his features so that he no longer appeared so frightening.

In the kitchen Vesta handed him a heavy wooden bucket. She was sure he had never lifted one before.

At the back of the Inn there was a bleating nanny-goat tied to a post, a number of young chickens scratching among a debris of rotten vegetables, feathers, and unidentifiable objects which smelt.

Someone, presumably the Inn-Keeper, had attempted half-heartedly to grow a few vegetables. They straggled forlornly among a multitude of sturdy and aggressive weeds.

Nature had done its best to compensate for the ugliness of it all with a briar bush brilliant with pink blossom, and everywhere they could survive small flowers turned their yellow, blue and white faces towards the sun.

Vesta led the way to the cascade.

When they reached it, the Count saw she was carrying a blackened pan, a dirty cloth and a knife she had taken from the kitchen table.

"Will you first fill the bucket and lift it clear of the cascade so that I can clean these?" she asked.

He did as she requested, watching her with a twinkle in his dark eyes as she scraped the pan until at least some of the ingrained grease and dirt was removed.

Her expression was serious as she concentrated on her work, and her long lashes were dark against her clear skin.

The sunshine percolating through the trees made her hair shine with golden lights and a soft breeze moved little tendrils of it against her neck.

She looked unreal, a nymph who might have strayed from the woods, a small goddess who had come down from Olympus to bemuse human beings.

"Your name is unusual," the Count remarked.

"Vesta was the Roman goddess of the hearth," Vesta replied.

"And thus goddess of fire," he added.

She did not answer and he asked:

"Is there any fire in your veins? Most English women are as cold as the snow on the mountains!"

"How many English women do you know?" Vesta asked. "If we appear cold and reserved as a race, it is because we have self-control . . . and pride."

"I was not talking about the English as a race," the Count answered, "but of English women and yourself in particular."

"Why should you be interested in what I feel?"

Vesta spoke truculently, her blue eyes wary as if she suspected he had some ulterior motive in speaking in such a manner.

"Naturally I am interested in the wife of my reigning Prince," the Count answered disarmingly.

"Y . . . yes . . . of course," Vesta answered.

"And you have not answered my question. Is there any of your namesake's fire in your make-up?"

"I do not . . . think . . . I understand what . . . you are trying to say," Vesta faltered.

"I think you do," he replied. "Do you yearn to love and be loved? Could a man make the breath come quicker between those two soft lips? Could your eyes become warm with desire?"

For a moment Vesta could not believe she had heard

him correctly. The colour rose in her cheeks as she said stiffly:

"Your questions are quite unanswerable, Count, even if I accepted that you had the right to ask them."

The Count laughed softly.

Putting down the pan, Vesta washed out the cloth, wringing it in her small hands until it was possible to use it to polish the pan.

"Now, if you will be kind enough to refill the bucket!" she said coldly. "I would like to wash before I go to bed."

"Cleanliness being of course next to godliness," he said mockingly.

"And much more comfortable," she retorted.

"Of course, Ma'am," he agreed.

She was sure he was laughing at her efforts to provide them both with a meal.

"You did not expect to have to cook and clean for your first dinner in Katōna," he said.

She thought that perhaps he was trying to make their conversation more normal and bridge the awkwardness he had caused by his impertinent questions.

"No indeed!" Vesta answered. "I imagined I should be entertained with much ceremony in magnificent sur- roundings!"

"And you would have enjoyed that?"

"It would be exciting to be . . . important!"

The Count raised his eyebrows, and Vesta said:

"I have five sisters older than I am. I have always had to wear their outgrown gowns, sit in a carriage with my back to the horses and do all the jobs no-one else wishes to do!"

The Count laughed.

"So you thought being Royal would be all you had dreamt of in splendour, pomp and circumstance."

"In . . . a . . . way."

Vesta's head was bent over the pan she was polish- ing.

"When it happens you may be disappointed," the Count warned.

"Why should I?" Vesta enquired.

"You may find the anticipation more exciting than the reality!"

He paused before he continued:

"We have a fairy story in Katōna about a Princess who fell asleep for a hundred years to be awakened by a Prince with a kiss."

"That is the tale of 'The Sleeping Beauty'," Vesta exclaimed, "and it was written by a Frenchman."

She was pleased to show off her knowledge.

"I often think," the Count continued as if she had not spoken, "that the Princess might have disliked having to face the world again and regretted the loss of her dreams."

"But she fell in love with the Prince," Vesta protested.

"Is that the French version?" the Count enquired. "Perhaps the Katōnian story has a different ending."

Vesta was still.

"Perhaps the Prince . . . did not . . . wish to . . . kiss . . . her," she said without thinking.

Then the colour rose in her cheeks again and she asked herself how she could have been so indiscreet as to speak of anything so intimate to the Count.

She half turned away from him, angry and embarrassed by her impulsiveness in speaking without thinking.

She rinsed the cloth again and wrung it out almost fiercely.

As if he sensed her tension and understood it, the Count asked lightly:

"Can you really cook?"

"You shall answer that question after dinner," Vesta replied with an effort. "I must admit to preferring a better equipment for the task than this."

The Count lifted the heavy bucket which leaked with every step he took, and carried it back to the door of the Inn.

Just as they reached it the woman appeared with a dead hen, head down, in her hand.

She said something which sounded defiant, and the Count translated to Vesta.

"Our hostess says she has killed an old hen. Not

even for the Prince himself would she sacrifice one of her young ones."

"I am sure His Royal Highness would be most disappointed at such lack of patriotism!" Vesta smiled.

The woman passed by them into the kitchen.

"You would be more comfortable sitting in front of the fire, Count," Vesta suggested. "If I have any further need of your services I will ask for your help."

"You are very gracious," he said sarcastically, but he walked obediently into the other room.

Besides the dead hen, the woman had brought in a number of eggs. Some of them looked dirty and old, and Vesta was wise enough to crack them separately finding, as she had anticipated, that some were bad and extremely smelly.

Presently the Count heard laughter coming from the kitchen, and when Vesta suddenly appeared he said before she could speak:

"Something seems to be amusing you."

"Our hostess thinks it very funny when I find a bad egg and hold my nose!" she said. "We are getting on extremely well in sign language."

She held out her hand towards him.

"I want to be quite sure which of these mushrooms which I have found just outside the Inn are edible. I have the feeling that the red ones, although I am not certain, are poisonous."

"They are indeed!" The Count said. "They are Aminita Muscaria. They grow in pine forests, and even if they did not kill us we should certainly spend a very uncomfortable night."

"That is what I thought," Vesta answered. "And these?"

She held out two other mushrooms that were yellow with brown spots on them.

"Those are Suillus Elegans," the Count said, "and are used a great deal in Katona. In fact they are quite delicious if well cooked."

"That is a challenge!" Vesta retorted and went back into the kitchen.

It was nearly an hour later before she appeared with a dish in her hands and two plates. She put them down

on the table and ran back to the kitchen to fetch two
forks.

"I have cleaned them," she said reassuringly.

She divided the omelette with a spoon and put the
larger piece on a plate for the Count.

"Eat it quickly," she said, "while it is hot."

Her face was flushed from the fire and her fair hair
was curling round her forehead. She looked young and
very lovely. The Count regarded her for a long moment
before he seated himself and put his fork into the omelette.

One mouthful told him that it was in fact delicious.
Very light and golden brown on the outside, it contained the mushrooms sliced thin and cooked in goat's
milk before they had been folded into the eggs.

"I congratulate you!" the Count exclaimed. "I had
no idea you were so talented."

"Mama always said we must never ask a servant to
do anything we could not do as well ourselves. And actually I enjoy cooking."

"I cannot imagine the Chef in the Palace will welcome you into his kitchen," the Count said.

"There may still be opportunities for me to show my
skill," Vesta answered.

She was thinking as she spoke of the riding expedi-
tions which she had planned that she and the Prince
would take together. Then she remembered with something like a little stab in her heart, that he would prob-
ably not wish to go with her.

She finished her portion of the omelette and taking
the empty dish and her plate went back into the
kitchen.

When she returned she carried another dish and two
warm plates.

"More food?" the Count questioned in surprise.

He had found in a cupboard some bottles of the
rough wine which was the habitual drink of the peasants of Katóna. He had opened one and now he poured
out a glass for Vesta and one for himself.

"I am afraid the menu is somewhat limited," Vesta
smiled, her dimples showing at either side of her
mouth, "and I am not certain how your black bread

will react to such an English dish as this, but you can try it for yourself."

She put the dish down on the table. It smelt pleasantly of cheese and the Count helped himself.

Vesta had found in the dirty kitchen not only the black bread which she had expected, but a lump of goat's cheese which the Inn-Keeper's wife had obviously made some time ago.

It was very hard, but slicing it finely, adding a few onions which were growing outside and a little goat's milk, she managed to produce a pale imitation of an English toasted cheese.

She looked at the Count anxiously as he tried the first mouthful.

"Very good!" he said. "I hope one day you will ask me to dinner—when you are doing the cooking!"

"I do not think goat's cheese toasts very well," Vesta said critically. "At the same time as I am hungry I must admit I am enjoying it."

"And so am I," the Count said in all sincerity, "and I congratulate you, Ma'am. Few women, let alone a Princess, could have produced such an excellent meal at such short notice and with so few ingredients."

Vesta smiled at him and for the first time forgot her hatred.

"It is kind of you to be so complimentary," she said. "I must say if we die of food poisoning it will not be my fault. I cannot bear to think what the average guest at this Inn has to put up with."

"The people of Katōna are very clean as a rule," the Count answered, "but this is such an isolated place that they have few travellers and their usual customers only come in for a drink. In fact this woman's husband earns most of his money in the woods and the Inn is only a side line."

"I am sure not many people would wish to eat here," Vesta said.

"Not unless you were doing the cooking," the Count answered.

"I wondered what I would do if no-one came for me and I had to stay on at Jēno after my money ran out," Vesta said. "I thought I might have to work in the orange-groves to pay for my keep, but now I realise I could have obtained a job as a cook. I would like to try to make the egg and lemon sauce that I had on my fish at luncheon."

"I can see you are very practical," the Count remarked.

Vesta smiled.

"I wish that were true! Mama is always scolding me for having my head in the clouds."

"And what do you think about when it is up there?" the Count enquired.

It was dusk outside and the light in the small room with its dirty windows was dim. The fire cast deep shadows and somehow it was easy to talk without feeling antagonistic.

"So many . . . things," Vesta answered.

"Tell me what you were thinking as we rode through the woods today," the Count suggested.

Vesta knew that, if she told the truth, she would have to say she was thinking most of the time of the Prince. But he was not a subject she wished to discuss with the Count, so she answered quickly:

"When I was looking at the flowers, and I have never seen anything so beautiful, I thought that they must be alive . . . just as we . . . are."

She paused and continued, choosing her words carefully.

"So perhaps it is cruel to . . . pick them. When we do so and they die, it may be as painful to them as it is to us if we are killed . . . or murdered."

Her voice died away and now she was suddenly apprehensive. How could she have told her secret thoughts to the Count of all people?

She expected him to laugh, and as she waited for him to do so it was like anticipating a physical blow. She could almost feel the pain of it!

Instead he answered quietly.

"Some Buddhists believe that to be the truth—as they will not take life, so they will not pick flowers."

Vesta's eyes were alight as she looked at him across the table.

"I imagined that . . . only I . . . had thought of . . . that."

"I am sure that as people develop spiritually in themselves and grow wiser, they all in their own way discover the same fundamental truths," the Count replied.

Vesta was silent. She turned over what he had said in her mind and exclaimed:

"That is one of the . . . nicest things . . . anyone has ever said to me!"

Then as if she felt shy, she rose to her feet.

"I must go and . . . help with the . . . chicken for . . . tomorrow," she said almost incoherently and sped from the room.

It was a long time before she returned, but the Count could hear voices and laughter coming from the kitchen. Somehow the two women were making themselves mutually understood.

Vesta came back into the room accompanied by the Inn-Keeper's wife, a lighted taper in her hand.

"She wants to show me the way to my bedroom," Vesta said to the Count.

"I will bring up the bucket," he answered and went through the kitchen to fetch it.

When he came back they climbed the steep wooden staircase. The woman went first with the taper, Vesta following her.

"You are honoured," the Count said as they reached the landing. "Candles are treasured in this part of the world. People go to bed before it is dark."

"I am very grateful!" Vesta smiled.

There were only two bed-rooms upstairs. They were side by side and the rickety doors did not fit. Vesta followed the woman into the first one and realised why she needed the lighted candle.

There was no glass in the window, which was stuffed with rags and old sacks so there was no light and no air.

A bed-stead of rough unpolished wood stood against one wall, by the other there was a table holding a basin.

There was nothing else, not even a chair, and at a

glance Vesta could see that the blankets were not only full of holes but extremely dirty.

The Count poured some of the water into the basin and put the bucket on the floor.

"Good night, Ma'am," he said politely.

She thought, as he withdrew from the room in the light of the candle, that he was smiling unpleasantly.

She had forgotten her hatred of him while they had been eating the dinner she had cooked. But now it returned with a new force.

She was quite certain he was gloating over the fact that she would never have seen a room that was quite so unpleasant or horrible as this one.

It smelt of dust, dirt and the sweat of those who had used it. She was quite certain there would be fleas in the bed, if nothing worse!

The woman put the candle down on the table.

"Good night," she said.

She was smiling and she even dropped an awkward curtsey.

"Good night and thank you," Vesta replied.

The candlelight cast strange shadows on the ceiling. Vesta looked at the bed with horror. Then she crossed the room to the basin and washed her hands and face in the cold water.

It was only when her face was already wet that she looked apprehensively for a towel, and having seen it decided nothing would induce her to use it.

Instead she drew her handkerchief from her pocket and was wiping her face when there came a knock on the door.

"Who is it?" she asked nervously.

"I have brought you your things from my saddle-bag," the Count answered. "I thought you must have forgotten them."

"Oh yes, as a matter of fact I had," Vesta said. "Thank you for bringing them."

She opened the door and took the bundle from him.

"Good night, Ma'am," he said with a little bow, "I hope you sleep well."

"I hope, Count, you also enjoy a good night," she replied sweetly.

She shut the door and heard him go into the room next door. She held her little bundle containing her pretty nightgown and brushes closely in her arms.

She had no intention of undressing in this squalor. She was also aware that it was growing cold.

She could hear the Count moving about next door and suddenly she came to a decision. She sat down on the edge of the bed, but fearing the dirt of it would mark the skirt of her riding-habit, she put her black cloak under her.

She waited for what seemed to her a long time until there were no longer any sounds from the next room. Then she slipped off her small kid boots which undid at her ankles, and picking up everything she possessed including her brushes and nightgown she very quietly opened the door.

With her boots in her hand, fearful of every creak of the stairs, she moved as softly as she could down to the front room with the fire.

It was still burning because the Count had put a lot of wood on it. Vesta set down her possessions on one wooden settle and lying on the other covered herself with her black cloak.

It was uncomfortable not to have a pillow and after a moment she rose to put more wood on the fire, moving very quietly in case someone should hear her.

Then she slipped off her smart white braided jacket and rolled it up to make a pillow for her head, and lay down once again.

The seat was hard under her body, but the fire was warm and she suddenly realised she was very tired.

She had been through so much. The worry over her arrival, the agony and fear she had experienced on the ride, her battle with the Count, had all taken their toll.

She felt her eyelids closing and then almost before she was aware of it she was fast asleep.

A log falling in the fire brought Vesta back through layers of sleep to consciousness.

She opened her eyes and she saw she was not alone.

Sitting on the wooden settle on the other side of the hearth was the Count. He was looking at her and she felt hazily it was perhaps the penetrating look in his dark eyes which had awoken her.

She stared at him for a moment and then drowsily still half asleep she said:

"I ... thought ... you were an ... eagle but you ... saved ... me."

"An eagle?" he questioned in a deep voice.

"I was ... falling," she murmured.

Then her eyes closed again and she went back to her dreams.

Chapter Four

Vesta awoke and saw light percolating through the dirty windows. For a moment she could not remember where she was.

Then she saw the dying embers of the fire still glowing red, and opposite her, stretched out on the other wooden settle so that she had not noticed him at first, the Count was lying fast asleep.

Very gently, so as not to awaken him, she stood up.

Her hip felt numb from the hardness of the wood, but she was no longer tired and the deep sleep she had enjoyed all night had left her refreshed and full of energy.

She glanced down at the Count and saw once again that he had taken off his cravat and his shirt was open.

She turned her eyes away, feeling she should not stare at him while he was unconscious. At the same time she could not help noticing that when he was relaxed he looked much younger and less intimidating.

'Perhaps,' she told herself, 'it is because his eyes are closed.'

Carrying her thick cloak over her arm and taking up the parcel which contained her only possessions from the floor where the Count must have put it, she crept towards the stairs.

They creaked as she climbed them, but when she reached the top and looked back, the Count was still asleep.

She went into the bed-room which she had been given to sleep in.

It smelt worse, she thought, even than it had the

54

night before, and crossing the dark room she pulled away the rubbish which had been stuffed into the window and let in the first gleams of sunlight.

She was determined to tidy herself up before they set out once again on their journey. Perhaps today, she thought, they would reach Djilas and she had no wish to arrive looking like a gypsy.

Standing on the table was the basin of water in which she had washed the night before. The bucket was still half full.

She went to the window, saw that there was nothing below but bushes, and flung the dirty water out.

Then she undressed, but was careful to put her clothes not on the floor which could not have been scrubbed for years, but onto her cloak.

She washed in the cold water and felt it fresh and invigorating and dried herself on her nightgown.

'When I get to Djilas someone will lend me a nightgown until my luggage arrives,' she thought confidently.

Then she dressed again, brushed her hair and tried to arrange it as best she could with the aid of a small piece of cracked mirror she found fixed to the wall.

Then having put a little powder on her small nose she went downstairs.

This had all taken some time and she was not surprised to find the front room was empty. She went towards the kitchen and met the Count coming out from it. He had shaved and his cravat was round his neck once again.

"You got up early," he said.

"I wanted to tidy myself," she answered.

"You look very elegant," he replied, and she was not certain whether it was a compliment or a criticism.

The Inn-Keeper's wife was boiling them eggs for breakfast. Vesta was too late to prevent them being hard boiled, but she felt it would be churlish to complain.

The old hen which she had shown the woman how to cook the night before appeared to be tender and not unappetising. The onions and milk which Vesta had added to the pot had given it a flavour.

Vesta carved it from the bone and finding nothing

clean to pack it in, used the paper which had covered her nightgown.

There was no other food to supplement the chicken, but she hoped that perhaps they would come across orange trees such as they had seen on their way up the mountain or some other fruit which grew in such profusion near the valley.

The Count ate his breakfast of eggs and butterless black bread quickly and, although he did not say so, Vesta had the impression that he was anxious to be off.

"Have we far to go today?" she asked.

"It depends," he replied. "I have not been on this track for some time and naturally the snows and the torrents change it year by year until it becomes almost unrecognisable. We may have to make a detour."

She thought he was deliberately attempting to discourage her, and she was sure of it when he fetched the horses round to the front of the Inn and said:

"Are you quite certain you would not rather turn back, Ma'am?"

She had the feeling that he was teasing rather than taunting her, but she replied in all seriousness:

"As I have told you before I have every intention of reaching Djilas."

Even if she had wished to return, she knew she could not have faced again the terror of that ride across the barren rock.

The Count paid the Inn-Keeper's wife who was all smiles as she bade them goodbye.

Vesta held out her hand.

"Thank you very much," she said in her halting Katōnian.

The woman asked a question and Vesta looked at the Count, wishing him to translate it for her.

"Our hostess asks if you were comfortable last night," he said.

"Will you tell her that I was very comfortable," Vesta replied.

He raised his eyebrows and said in English:

"I thought you were truthful."

"It is the truth," Vesta replied. "I slept exceedingly well, as you know."

He conveyed literally what she had said and the woman clasped her hands together in pleasure, curtseying and obviously wishing them "God speed" on their journey.

She stood waving to them and Vesta waved back until they were out of sight.

"She did her best," she said almost as if she spoke to herself.

"You are very charitable," the Count remarked.

"It is what people try to do which matters," Vesta replied, "and it is a mistake to expect too much."

She remembered as she spoke what her father and mother had said about her and added almost to herself:

"We must never expect too much."

"As a safeguard against being disappointed," the Count said and there was a touch of irony in his voice.

Vesta did not answer. She was telling herself that when she arrived at Djilas she must not expect too much of the Prince.

Perhaps he would not like her very much at first, but if they could only be friendly with each other, then one day love might come. It would be hard to be married without love.

The path under the trees was much the same as it had been the day before. The sun was rising and there was every likelihood of it becoming very hot.

Vesta untied the ribbons from under her chin and balanced her hat in front of her.

Then she found this was uncomfortable and finally she tied the two ribbons together at their extreme ends and let her hat hang down her back. She also took off her gloves and put them into her jacket pocket.

She knew her mother would not have approved of her appearing so unconventionally garbed. But here among the trees there was no-one to see her, and she decided later on she might even take off her jacket.

She began to understand why the Count found it more comfortable to ride without a cravat round his neck.

The horses plodded on neither hastening or slowing their pace, keeping up an even gait in a manner which showed they were used to long journeys and had no intention of over-exerting themselves.

Vesta was soon lost in her day-dreams, finding the golden sunshine seeping through the leaves so lovely that it made her think of the stories from mythology that she had read about Greece. She felt they must also apply to Katōna.

She was beginning to feel hungry when at last the Count drew the horses to a halt.

"I have the feeling," he said, "that we should eat that so-called chicken you cooked last night before it grows even older in the saddle-bag."

"I admit to being quite hungry," Vesta said.

She slipped down from her horse, knowing there was no need to do anything but let the animal roam loose, and then she gave a little cry of delight.

The trees here were thinner than in other parts of the forest, and where the sunshine pierced through there was everywhere grass and a few flowers.

Amongst them she saw some small red strawberries, the *fraises de bois* of the Mediterranean. She ran towards them excited as a child.

"Strawberries!" she exclaimed. "I felt certain we should find them here."

She tasted one. It was sweet and warm from the sunshine. Then she picked a handful and carried them to where the Count had sat down with his back to the trunk of a tree, the sliced chicken at his side.

Vesta put the strawberries down on the paper in which it had been wrapped and said:

"I will find some more later. Let us eat the chicken first."

"If I were a better naturalist," the Count said, "I would doubtless be able to find you some wild lettuce. I see that my education has been sadly neglected when it comes to the flora of my own country."

"I was thinking when I first arrived," Vesta said, "that I must learn more about herbs that grow in Katōna."

"Why?" he enquired.

"Mama is very knowledgeable on such subjects as herbal medicines, salves and lotions," Vesta replied.

"We have a herb garden at home. It was laid out in the reign of Henry VIII."

She took a bite of the chicken and went on:

"Now this would have been much improved if I could have found some Basil. I wonder what the right word for it is in Katōnian."

"You will have to find a book on cookery," the Count said.

"Is there a large library at the Palace?" Vesta asked.

"Quite a comprehensive one," the Count replied. "The late Prince Andreas, His Royal Highness's father, was a great reader."

"That will be wonderful for me," Vesta said, "but first I must improve my knowledge of your language."

"You obviously intend to settle in and stay here," the Count remarked.

A flush rose to her cheeks as she said angrily:

"Are you still intent on sending me home? You are very persistent, but I am as determined as you are that nothing will induce me to leave."

"Nothing?" he enquired.

"Only if the Prince was dead," she answered. "Do you imagine the Revolutionaries might kill him?"

The Count shrugged his shoulders. Then he asked:

"Would it sadden you very much?"

The question was a surprise and Vesta replied:

"Naturally . . . I should be . . . upset."

"Because you had lost a husband you had never seen?"

She would have answered him, but she had the feeling that he was deliberately trying to make her feel uncomfortable.

"I think, Count," she said, "that once again you are encroaching on matters which do not concern you."

She tried to speak with great dignity but it was rather difficult when they were sitting side by side in the middle of the wood sharing pieces of chicken, and she was conscious that her hair had been blown by the breeze around her cheeks.

There was a glint of amusement in his eyes before he said:

"You are very severe, Ma'am."

"I am trying to behave . . . correctly," Vesta replied, "and you are not making it . . . very easy for . . . me."

"Then I must apologise in all sincerity," he answered.

For once she thought he was not speaking mockingly, and looking away from him she said:

"I cannot help feeling lonely and a little . . . homesick. When the ship sailed away it was my last link with England, and I am trying . . . hard to like everything in Katōna since it will in future be my . . . home."

She tried to speak unemotionally but there was a perceptible quiver in her voice. After a moment the Count said in a tone which he had never used to her before:

"You must forgive me if my attitude has made things more difficult for you than they would have been otherwise."

Vesta had always found it hard to bear a grudge when people apologised for anything they had said or done.

She gave the Count a shy little smile. Then she rose to her feet saying:

"I will try and find more strawberries. I am sure there must be some over there in the sunshine."

She moved away from him and he watched her as she went from the shade of the trees out into the sunshine where she had noticed there were flowers.

She was right: for nestling beneath their green leaves there was quite a profusion of the small red berries.

She picked a handful, and when she could hold no more and thought she had best take them back to the Count she turned round.

She had wandered quite some way from the trees and was standing on a little plateau covered with flowers which descended sharply down to the trees below.

As she started to walk back towards the wood there was a hissing noise in the grass and in front of her she saw a long black snake.

She was frozen into stillness, realising she could not move backwards and it would be almost impossible to pass the reptile without it striking at her.

Almost involuntarily she gave a little cry and realised that the Count had risen to his feet.

"What is it?" he called.

The snake was hissing aggressively, and now Vesta thought that to call out might incite it further.

Vaguely at the back of her mind she remembered it was best not to move when one encountered a snake, but to stand still. She therefore stood rigid, holding the strawberries in her hand, her eyes on the snake.

It seemed to resent her presence, raising its head, its forked tongue flicking in and out of its mouth, its yellow eyes regarding her balefully.

She could see the movement of the scales on its back and she had a feeling that at any moment it would dart towards her and strike at her ankle.

The Count had come to the edge of the wood. He saw at once what was keeping her silent, and with a swiftness she could hardly believe possible he ran to his horse and drew something from the saddle-bag.

Then he was moving purposefully towards her.

"Keep still, do not move!" he commanded.

At the sound of his voice the snake turned its head towards him and then there was the shattering report of a pistol as the Count shot it dead. The noise echoing and re-echoing round the mountains and across the valley.

Vesta saw its head was shattered but its tail was still thrashing in the air. The Count stepped over it and picking her up swung her over the still writhing reptile to safety.

He put her down and looked at her pale face.

"Are you all right?" he asked. "It did not touch you?"

"No . . . I am all . . . right," Vesta answered and turning she walked away from him.

'I must not show emotion,' she told herself severely. 'I must be calm. He will think it ill-bred if I am afraid of a snake.'

The sound of the pistol-shot was still ringing in her ears, and when she reached her horse she hung onto the saddle as if for support. The Count came back towards her.

He went to his own horse and drew from his saddle-bag a red silk belt such as she had seen the natives in Jēno wearing.

He put it on and slipped the pistol into it and she knew it was intended to carry either pistols or a knife.

The Count came to her side.

"I should have anticipated there would be snakes at this time of the year," he said angrily. "It was criminally careless of me, first to let you wander about without warning you, and secondly not to have been wearing a pistol. It will not happen again."

"Was that snake . . . poisonous?" Vesta asked in what she hoped was a calm voice.

"As a matter of fact it was!" the Count answered. "There are many snakes in Katōna some of them quite harmless, but a bite from one of the black ones sometimes proves fatal."

As he spoke he picked her up and put her on the saddle.

"We had best hurry on towards civilization," he said. "We have had enough of the other sort these last twenty four hours to last us both for a life-time."

He mounted and rode on at a quicker pace. Now the trees were interspersed with rocks and Vesta noticed that the Count seemed to be looking upwards and around him as if he was searching for something.

As the path grew wider she rode up beside him.

"What are you looking for?" she asked.

"Nothing in particular," he answered, "but it is not always wise to draw attention to oneself in this particular region. It has a somewhat unhealthy reputation. A pistol shot can be heard for miles away."

"What do you mean by unhealthy?" Vesta asked.

Then even as she spoke she saw a number of men scrambling down towards them through the trees.

The Count's hand went towards his pistol, but even as he touched it he realised there were at least a dozen men advancing towards them and he was outnumbered.

The men drew nearer and Vesta saw they were roughly dressed in native white cotton tunics and over them sleeveless coats of sheep-skin or fur. They were

bare-headed and the majority of them had greasy untidy hair, long moustaches or beards.

They all of them carried stout poles in their hands
and each man had a huge knife stuck into a belt not
unlike the Count's.

They came nearer until the Count and Vesta who
had drawn their horses to a standstill were encircled.

"What do you want?" the Count asked.

The man who replied spoke with a dialect which was
quite impossible for Vesta to understand. But whatever
it was the Count protested hotly.

"We are travellers doing no harm. All we ask is that
we can proceed in peace."

Again the man spoke harshly. He was an unpleas-
ant-looking individual, Vesta thought: he had a notice-
able squint and a deep scar running from his cheekbone
to the corner of his mouth giving him almost a grotesque
appearance.

One man stepped forward to take hold of the bridle
of Vesta's horse, another did the same to the Count's.

"What is ... happening?" Vesta asked in a frightened tone.

"They insist on taking us to see their Chief," the
Count replied in English.

"Their Chief?" Vesta enquired in surprise.

"They are Brigands," the Count said grimly. "I am
afraid there is nothing we can do but acquiesce to their
demands."

Two men appeared and drew large dirty handkerchiefs from their belts. One of them advanced towards
Vesta. As she shrank back from the thought of him
touching her, the Count spoke sharply and raising his
hands took his cravat from round his neck.

"They wish to blindfold us," he said, "but I have
told them that you are my wife and that no-one must
touch you but me. I will therefore blindfold you myself."

He bent towards her without dismounting and put
his cravat over her eyes, tying it behind her head.

"Try not to be frightened," he said softly.

But she knew he was only trying to encourage her
and that the position in which they found themselves

was likely to be extremely unpleasant if not dangerous.

She imagined that the Count himself also was being blindfolded, and then she heard his horse led ahead in front of hers and there was nothing she could do but hold onto her saddle and wonder what was going to happen.

As they went the men said very little amongst themselves.

Since she could not see them, their silence was more uncanny than if they had chattered away and she had tried to understand what they were saying.

They left the path on which she and the Count had been travelling and were now climbing steadily up the side of the mountain.

They were zig-zagging, Vesta thought to avoid trees; but after perhaps half an hour the trees clearly had been left behind because now there was the sound of the horses' hooves on rock.

She wondered fearfully whether there was a sudden drop at one side of her such as there had been before.

The Count did not speak to her, but she was vividly conscious of him being led ahead. Once indeed he did start to talk to the Head man who had given the orders in the first place.

Vesta recognised the word "money" and guessed that the Count was offering to pay for their freedom.

'It must be for ransom they are taking us,' she thought.

The Brigand replied sharply and briefly, and although Vesta did not understand she was sure he had replied that it was up to the Chief to decide what should be done.

On and on they went, climbing all the time.

The sun was hot on Vesta's bare head and on her hands. But now she could feel a cool breeze and was sure that it came from the tops of the mountains.

'We must be very high by now,' she thought.

Yet still they climbed, even the ponies grunting a little with the exertion, and some of their escort were breathing heavily.

Hours must have gone by and still they climbed, until finally there was a sharp word of command, the horses were brought to a standstill and Vesta felt strong hands from which she shrank drawing her from the saddle.

She stood uncertain and indecisive, wondering whether she could take off the bandage. Then with a sense of relief she heard the Count say:

"Give me your hand."

She groped for his and found it.

"Will ... they ... hurt us?" she asked, her fingers trembling.

"I hope not," he replied.

She had the feeling that he was unsure and worried.

They were led forward, Vesta feeling the way with her feet and praying that she would not suddenly trip up and fall. Then someone spoke and the Count said to Vesta:

"We may take off our bandages."

She undid hers quickly and found that at last she was able to see.

It took her a moment or two to adjust her eyes, not to the sunshine that she had expected, but to the dimness of a cave.

It was an enormous cavern hewn out of solid rock, dark and grey. It was lit by light coming through a distant opening and two flaring torches.

What arrested Vesta's attention more than anything else were the people surrounding them.

She and the Count were standing in the very centre of the cave and staring at them were perhaps twenty or thirty men and women all dressed roughly in the same style as their captors.

There were too, she noticed, a number of small, dark-haired, unhealthy-looking children. While the women were so unprepossessing that it was difficult to realise that they were of the same sex as herself.

But above all her gaze was riveted by a man who was obviously the Chief.

He was a big man, bigger than the others, and there were grey streaks in his hair. His eyes were bright and shrewd, while his face was deeply scarred as if from many fights and his nose having been broken had been badly set.

He spoke harshly, but the Count replied coolly and in even tones, and Vesta knew he was explaining that they were ordinary travellers intent on their own business.

The Count made a gesture towards her and it was clear that he was saying that she was his wife.

The Chief made a joke at which he laughed heartily, while the Count did not smile. Then the Chief said something to his followers and they murmured amongst themselves.

One or two of them put their hands towards the knives in their belts and for the first time Vesta was really afraid.

The Count became very eloquent.

Now she knew he was threatening, cajoling, pleading, but the answer to everything he said was definitely unsatisfactory. Again Vesta heard the word "money" which she recognised.

She had the strange feeling that it was not of interest to the Chief.

Finally when the argument seemed to have gone on for a long time with no satisfactory conclusion, the Count obviously asked if he might explain what had happened to Vesta. The Chief nodded.

The Count turned towards her and she saw an expression in his face which made her tremble.

"What do they intend to . . . do to . . . us?" she asked.

"I am to die," he answered. "They say we have violated their territory and therefore they intend to kill me."

She tried to speak but no word would come. Then he said:

"They will spare your life if you will become the wife—which is a polite word for it—of the Head man who brought us here. He is the brother of the Chief."

For a moment Vesta could not take in what the Count was saying.

Then remembering the man with the squinting eye and the scar on his cheek, she said quietly in a voice which surprisingly did not tremble:

"You will kill me."

It was not a question, it was a statement of fact. The Count looking into her eyes answered.

"Of course."

"How will you . . . do it?" Vesta asked.

"They have taken my pistol," he answered, "but I have a knife in my belt."

She drew in a deep breath.

"There is a place I . . . believe between the . . . breasts . . ." she whispered.

"I know it."

"I would not wish to . . . scream in front . . ."

"No, of course not."

She thought to herself this could not be happening. It could not be true! Strangely enough she felt quite calm. It was as if the shock had taken away all feeling and it did not matter that she must die.

"I will ask them," the Count said, "if I can say goodbye to you. They will expect protestations of love and dramatics. It is what they themselves enjoy."

He turned his head towards the Chief. It took him some time to say what he wanted and the Chief's reply was equally voluble. The Count turned back to Vesta.

"He has given us three minutes in which to say our farewells," he said. "What I want you to do is undo your jacket and then put your arms round my neck. You will hide the movement of my hand as I draw the knife from my belt. When I am ready I will kiss you and strike at the same time. Do you understand?"

"I understand," she answered, her eyes on his.

She undid the buttons of her jacket and then moving close against him she put her arms round his neck.

It was the only time she had ever been close to a man and somehow she could not realise it would be the last time as well as the first.

She could feel the Count's heart beating and she also knew that as one arm encircled her his other hand was fumbling at his waist.

She felt him draw something from his belt.

"We must keep talking," he said, "they will not understand what we say and they will imagine that we are being affectionate."

"How will they . . . kill you?" she asked.

"With their knives," the Count answered. "When one dies it is of little consequence how it is contrived."

"You will be quite ... certain that I am ... dead before they do ... anything to you?" she whispered. "I could not face being left ... alive ... with them."

"I promise that you will die," he answered. "There will be no pain."

The Chief spoke and Vesta knew he was telling them they had little time.

Everyone in the cave had drawn nearer to them. The men, women and children were all watching and now there was a tense silence as if they savoured the drama taking place.

"Are you ready?" the Count asked.

"I am ... ready," Vesta replied.

"Then put your lips on mine," he said and she felt him draw back his hand taut against his chest.

It was level with her own breast and she knew that in one second the knife would pierce her skin in the spot which, if applied properly, meant instant death.

She drew in her breath. With her whole being she prayed she would be brave and not cry out.

'Help me ... God!'

Her arms tightened round the Count's neck.

Then a sudden scream shattered the silence in the cave. It was so sharp, so shrill, that almost instinctively both Vesta and the Count turned to see what was happening.

It was a woman who had screamed and she was pointing not at them but at a child standing at their feet.

It was a little boy of perhaps eighteen months old, under-sized and emaciated, but at this moment crimson in the face, his eyes bulging from their sockets. It was quite obvious he was struggling uneffectively for breath.

For a moment everyone stared while the woman screamed and screamed, her voice echoing and re-echoing.

Then swiftly, almost without thinking, Vesta took her arms from the Count's neck and seizing the child picked him up in her arms and turned him upside down.

For a moment she held him suspended and then something fell from his mouth to clatter onto the floor.

It was a pebble!

The woman had stopped screaming as Vesta had picked up the child, so the sound of the pebble falling on the stone floor was clearly heard by everyone. The woman who had screamed bent forward to pick it up.

She held it in her hand, and then as Vesta placed the child back on his feet he started to cry—the loud and protesting roar of a small boy who has been frightened.

His mother ignored him and held the pebble out in her hand for everyone to see. Then she went down on her knees in front of Vesta and kissed her hand.

There were tears running down her face and she was saying something in a broken voice over and over again.

Vesta looked at the Count and as she did so a babble of noise broke out in the cave.

The Chief Brigand came towards them. He spoke to the people and they were silent as he burst into a flood of words which Vesta could not understand.

But she could see he was smiling and was bowing towards her.

The woman was still kissing her hand, while the child was being comforted by another woman who had picked him up in her arms.

The Count spoke quietly.

"The Chief says you have saved the life of his only son. He has eight daughters but this is his heir."

The Count's voice deepened and Vesta could hear the relief in it as he went on:

"We are no longer his prisoners nor are we to die. We are his guests and there is to be a feast in our honour."

Vesta looked at him in a bewildered way. Then she swayed slightly and the Count put his arm round her shoulder.

"It is all right," he said quickly, "it is all over. You have saved us both."

Vesta took a deep breath and the numb feeling which had made her feel everything was a dream began

to pass. Even now she could not realise how near she
had been to death.

The women were bustling about receiving instructions from the Chief.

"What is happening?" Vesta asked.

"They will kill a goat," the Count said, "and if we
were near to death before, I can assure you that when
we eat it we shall be even nearer."

He was trying, Vesta knew, to speak lightly to allevi-
ate the horror of what had happened.

"I expect you would like to sit down," he said, "but
this place seems most inadequately furnished."

He looked round the big cave and then Vesta saw
there were seats of a sort placed round the walls and
covered with the skins of animals.

But before the Count could lead her to one of them
a woman came to her side.

She was young, ugly and dirty, and her hair was
straggling down her face. She was very thin and under-
nourished and when Vesta looked down at the baby in
her arms, she thought for a moment it was dead.

It was a very small, emaciated little baby, and its
face seemed blue.

"What is she saying?" Vesta asked the Count.

"She asks if you will help her," the Count answered,
"but there is nothing you can do."

"How do you know there is nothing?" Vesta
enquired.

"It would be a mistake to try to do anything," he replied. "The child will die anyway, and they might say it
was your fault."

"But I must help it if I can. What does she say is
wrong?" Vesta asked.

"I have told you to leave her alone," the Count said
sharply. "You have performed one miracle, do not
press your luck too hard!"

Vesta straightened herself and moved away from his
protecting arm.

"I wish to know what this woman is saying to me."

She met his eyes as she spoke and once again it was
a contest of wills between them.

"Please translate," Vesta said firmly.

"Are you commanding me?" he asked with a twist of his lips.

"If necessary," she replied. "Brigands or not, they will be my people."

"Very well, Ma'am," he said with a sigh. "If you bring the wrath of the Chief down on our heads again, there will be nothing I can do about it."

He turned almost impatiently towards the woman.

"She says," he translated into English, "that the baby is four days old and she has no milk. She asks if you can help her as you helped her sister. She especially wants you to save this baby as it is a boy too. Now will you admit there is nothing you can do?"

Once again he was jeering at her, Vesta thought.

"Ask the woman if she has been trying to feed the baby."

The Count did as she asked.

"She says they have spooned some goat's milk into its mouth, but it will not swallow it."

"Of course it will not at that age," Vesta said.

The other women were standing round trying to understand what was happening.

"Tell one of those women," Vesta said to the Count, "to get some fresh goat's milk and ask them if possible to put it into a clean pot."

"I imagine that is very unlikely," he said dryly.

However he gave Vesta's instructions to a woman who hurried away.

When she was gone Vesta touched the child's hands. They were very cold, yet it was alive and still breathing, although she had the feeling it would not be for long.

The woman came back with the goat's milk. It was warm from the animal. Vesta drew one of her gloves from the pocket of her jacket.

"I want a spoon," she said to the Count.

One was procured for her and she spooned the milk into the first finger of the glove.

She was watched by the women and now the men began to crowd round as well.

"I hope to God," the Count said in a low voice, "you know what you are doing."

Vesta ignored him. The glove was of soft suede and when she had filled the finger with milk, she took a brooch from the front of her blouse and pierced a hole in the tip of the finger.

Then she dipped it into the goat's milk and pressed it to the baby's mouth.

For a moment it paid no attention. Its mouth opened and it gave a feeble cry. Vesta pressed the glove a little further in and now the baby's lips closed on it.

Very feebly it gave a little suck, then it sucked again. It seemed as if everyone held their breath until it was sucking at the glove finger as if at last it had found the food it needed.

It was then that Vesta was besieged! It appeared that everyone in the whole cave wanted her help and her guidance for their children.

The Count created some order out of the tumult, making one woman speak at a time and insisting on the others taking their turn.

"Tell me," she said to him, "what do these people eat?"

"Meat mostly," he answered. "Their men hunt in the hills for goat and bear to which they are very partial, and I believe they have a traditional dish made of porcupine."

"Do they get any vegetables or fruit?" Vesta asked.

"I imagine they see no necessity for them," the Count replied.

Vesta made him tell the mothers that someone was to go down to the valley and bring back a sack of oranges, and that every child was to have at least one a day.

She told them to eat the wild strawberries, to keep lemons always in the cave and be quite certain that they had enough olives when the harvest was over to see them through winter, so that every child could have a few drops of olive oil every day.

They listened open-mouthed. Then the Count said:

"One of the women, who seems more intelligent than the rest, asks what they can do in the winter when there is no fruit to be had? I imagine the majority of them suffer from scurvy of some sort."

"Will you tell them," Vesta replied, "to put a handful of pine needles in a large pot of boiling water. They are to leave it for an hour and then drink five cupfuls of it a day."

"Are you sure that will be effective?" the Count asked in surprise.

"It was a Russian who told my mother that is what they do in Siberia," Vesta answered.

He gave the information to the mothers and they nodded their heads. Vesta knew they would follow out her orders.

"They must be able to get honey," she said to the Count.

"If they bother to gather it there is plenty in the woods," he answered. "You can imagine with flowers like ours there are swarms of bees in their hundreds."

"Tell the women the men are not to be cowards and they must collect honey for the children. Say they must jeer at them if they are frightened of being stung!"

The women roared with laughter at this.

"Tell them the children are to have at least three spoonfuls of honey a day all the year round, and they can put honey into the pine-needle drink if they find it nasty."

There were so many questions that Vesta began to get very tired, and at last the Count took her by the arm and drew her away to one of the seats near the wall.

"I have told them the Physician's Consulting Room is closed for the evening!" he said.

The women chattered amongst themselves, obviously accepting his decision, and now they were busy arranging a table in the middle of the room where the feast was to take place.

"How do you know all these things?" the Count asked.

"I told you I was interested in herbs," she answered.

"I cannot believe that anyone who looks like you would have so much knowledge and save both our lives."

"It was luck," she said simply. "The same thing happened to one of my nieces. Her father did exactly what

I did to that child and what was stuck in her throat fell out. Afterwards she was perfectly all right."

"Perhaps we were not meant to die," the Count said, "not at the moment at any rate!"

"Will they let us . . . go?" she asked a little apprehensively.

"We shall have to stay here tonight," he answered. "The feast will go on a long time and it would be insulting to leave too quickly as it is being given in our honour. Tomorrow I am certain the chief will keep his word and we shall be free."

"I hope . . . so," Vesta said in a small voice.

The Count put his hand over hers. It was strangely comforting.

Chapter Five

The feast was obviously being enjoyed by everyone from the oldest Brigand down to the smallest child who could feed itself.

Vesta had tried not to look when the goat, which had been roasted whole over a fire outside, was carried in. It looked horrible, she felt, with its head still attached to it.

It was placed in the middle of a long table and the Chief Brigand helped his guests, himself and his immediate family, and then the others hacked away with their knives at whatever portion they fancied.

Vesta looked with horror at the heaped plate of meat which was set down in front of her.

Fortunately she was seated next to the Count who was on the right of their host.

"Chew the meat," he said softly, "then remove it from your mouth and feed it to the dogs. You will find quite a number of them under the table."

His eyes twinkled as he went on:

"It may not be good manners, but that is something which is in somewhat short supply amongst our hosts."

That was certainly true. The Brigands stuffed the meat into their mouths with both hands, chewed it with relish, and belched when it suited them.

They were of course waited on by the women, and Vesta was the only female who was seated all through the meal.

She was glad that she was not near to the Headman with the squint eye who had asked for her as his wife.

She was well aware that during the meal he was

looking at her with an expression that made her shudder, and because she was afraid, she moved a little nearer to the Count.

He looked at her as if to enquire what was perturbing her.

"You will not leave me ... alone, will you?" she asked.

He saw the Headman watching them and realised why she was upset.

"You need not be afraid," he replied quietly, "I promise that he shall not come near you."

This was reassuring, at the same time Vesta could not help a tremor of fear every time she looked up and realised that the Headman was staring at her, even when he stuffed large portions of the meat into his mouth.

Red wine such as they had drunk at the Inn circulated freely and soon the laughter grew louder. Vesta guessed that it was a good thing she could not understand the jokes, for she was sure they were extremely coarse.

She drank a little of the wine and ate the dark black bread, which despite its somewhat acid taste was quite edible.

She even enjoyed the goat's cheese which was not as old and hard as the piece she had tried to cook the night before.

At last when she was beginning to feel very tired, the bones which was all that remained of the goat were taken away from the table and Vesta knew with relief that the feast was over.

The Chief said something to the Count and he turned to Vesta to say:

"We are indeed honoured. The Chief and his wife are giving up their own cave to us. I have told them it is unnecessary, but he insists."

The favour however was not so acceptable when Vesta saw the cave.

It was quite small, leading off the main cavern where they had eaten.

Over the opening there was stretched bear-skin and inside a large bed consisted entirely of the furs of animals piled one on top of another. There were no other furnishings.

Light and air came only from the large cave, until the Chief Brigand's wife brought in a small flaring torch of birchwood which she thrust into an iron holder set into the wall.

"She says it will burn only for perhaps ten minutes," the Count said dryly "so we best arrange ourselves for sleep."

With many good night greetings, the Chief Brigand and his wife withdrew from the cave and the bear-skin fell behind them.

Vesta looked at the bed apprehensively. The Count saw the expression on her face and said:

"I think the only hope is to spread out your cloak. I do not fancy the fur blankets and I am sure you do not either."

Remembering the dirt of the Brigands and of their women, Vesta shuddered.

The Count took Vesta's thick cloak and laid it over the bed so that the wide hem covered where their heads would rest and only their feet would actually rest on the animal skins.

"It may seem unconventional for us to be here together," the Count said in a quiet voice, "but I imagine you would not wish me to suggest that I sleep in the main cave?"

Vesta thought of the Headman and the way he had watched her all through the meal and shuddered.

"No ... please ... please, do not ... leave me," she begged.

"I cannot suggest," the Count went on, "that I should sleep in a chair all night because there is none. And quite frankly, Ma'am, I do not fancy the floor."

"No, of course not," Vesta said. "We can both lie on the bed now that you have covered it with my cloak. There is no question of undressing."

She shivered as she spoke. After the heat of the outside cave she could now feel the cold which obviously came from the snow on the mountains.

'We must be very high,' she thought.

Then feeling a little shy she climbed onto the bed

and keeping well to one side of it lay back against her cloak.

"The bed is very soft," she told the Count. "I wonder how much the furs on which we are lying are worth."

"Are you thinking of asking for them to be made into a cloak for you?" he teased.

"Indeed not," Vesta replied. "At the same time I was wondering why the Brigands do not sell some of the furs they acquire and buy furniture."

"I imagine they are quite happy as they are," the Count answered, "and think that they are living in luxury. They are not really Katōnians—they are Albanians who have fled from their country and the cruelty of the Turkish conquerors to settle here. I have heard about them for years, but fortunately I have never encountered them until now."

"Have they killed . . . many people, as they would have killed . . . you?" Vesta asked.

"If travellers wander onto what they consider their territory, I imagine their lives are forfeit," the Count said. "We were however unfortunate in that they heard my pistol-shot when I killed the snake. Otherwise we might have passed by and they would have had no idea that we were there."

As he spoke he lowered himself carefully onto the bed as Vesta had done. He lay on the extreme edge of his side of it and there was a large gap between them.

"I should try and sleep," he said as he settled himself uncomfortably. "I imagine that the Brigands have taken us considerably out of our way and we have a long ride ahead of us tomorrow."

"I am very tired," Vesta said. "I am sure I will sleep."

As she spoke she thought of how except, as the Count had said, by a miracle, they might both have been dead at this moment. Where would the Brigands have buried them? Even the thought of their touching her dead body made her shiver.

"Are you cold?" the Count asked.

"Not really," she answered, "I was shivering at the thought that we might be . . . dead."

"Forget it!" the Count said sharply.

As he spoke the torch flickered and went out leaving only the fragrance of birch-wood.

It was now very dark in the cave except, as Vesta's eyes grew accustomed to the darkness, she could see beneath the bear-skin a light from the outer cavern.

'I will try not to think of what has happened,' she told herself, 'but of the flowers, and the sunshine coming through the trees.'

She shut her eyes and tried to forget the Count was lying beside her. Then suddenly there was a faint noise.

"What is . . . that?" she asked nervously.

"Rats, I expect," the Count answered.

He spoke casually, but Vesta gave a little scream and turning wildly towards him, clutched hold of his coat and hid her face against his shoulder.

"Do not let . . . them come . . . near me! Keep them . . . away!" she cried frantically.

After a second's astonishment, the Count put his arms round her.

"It is all right," he said soothingly, "I will not let them hurt you."

"They might . . . run over . . . me," Vesta whispered, "I cannot . . . bear it."

She was rigid with fear, holding onto his lapel, hiding her face, but was listening intently.

Then suddenly she raised her head a little and said accusingly:

"You are . . . laughing!"

"Today I thought you were the bravest, most gallant woman I have ever met in my whole life," the Count said in a deep voice. "You faced death without crying, without a murmur; you stood still when you expected a reptile to attack you; and yet now—you are afraid of a rat!"

"I cannot . . . help it," Vesta murmured, "I am . . . humiliated at letting you see what a . . . coward I am . . . but they . . . terrify me."

"I would never think you a coward, whatever frightened you," the Count said. "As I have said, I do not believe that any woman could have been more magnificent when you were ready to die at my hand."

Vesta did not answer and after a moment he realised she was crying.

"What have I said? How have I upset you?" he asked, and now there was a deep concern in his voice.

"It is . . . because you are so . . . kind," Vesta sobbed. "It is easier to be . . . brave when I am . . . hating you."

The Count tightened his arms round her.

"You have been through so much!" he said gently, "but it is over now. Thanks to you we are alive."

He knew she was fighting for self-control and after a few moments she released her hold on his lapel. Drawing a handkerchief from her jacket, she wiped her eyes.

"I am . . . ashamed of . . . myself."

"There is no need to be," the Count answered.

"You have . . . said that you think I am . . . brave," Vesta said in a very low voice, "but I am not . . . really. I lied to you . . . yesterday when I told you I felt . . . sick from being on . . . land."

She gave a little gulp as if it was hard to be honest.

"It was . . . really that I felt . . . faint because I was so . . . frightened when we rode over the . . . barren rocks. I have always been . . . afraid of . . . heights."

The words sounded piteous and now Vesta hid her face once again.

"It is extremely brave of you to tell me the truth," the Count said, "but I must admit I suspected it was that which had upset you."

He stared into the darkness and said quietly:

"We all have an Achilles heel. Perhaps one day you will discover mine."

"There is something of which you are afraid?" Vesta asked curiously.

"Of course," he answered, "but I have not the courage to tell you what it is."

There was silence for a moment and then Vesta faltered.

"You . . . will not . . . tell the . . . Prince when we reach Djilas that I was . . . afraid of the height or that I . . . cried just now?"

"You do not wish him to know?" the Count asked.

"No, please do not ... tell him," Vesta pleaded. "Mama told me that it is very ill-bred to show emotion of any sort and that Royalty are always brave, even when anarchists throw bombs at their carriages or fire pistols at them."

"And what about the other types of emotion?" the Count asked. "Do you intend to suppress them too?"

"What sort of emotions?" Vesta asked.

"Love is of course the most important," the Count replied.

There was silence.

"Mama said," Vesta answered in a very small voice, "that I must not ... expect love."

"And yet you hope for it!" the Count said gently.

Vesta drew in a deep breath.

How did he know she wondered that she hoped and prayed that the Prince would love her and she could love him?

Then she knew that this was not the sort of conversation she should be having with a strange man who was the Prince's friend and part of his entourage.

"I am sure," she answered slowly, "that Mama would think it very ... wrong of me to talk to you in such an ... intimate manner. I know too she would be very ... shocked at our lying here ... together, although I do not see what else we can do about it."

As Vesta spoke she eased herself free of the Count's encircling arms, to move back to her own side of the bed.

"There are two things I think you should consider," the Count said, "first that the circumstances in which we find ourselves are definitely exceptional, and secondly that your mother being many miles away could hardly be expected to cope with the rats in this cave."

Even as he spoke, Vesta heard once again the scrabbling that had frightened her before.

Without thinking, instinctively she threw herself once again against the Count holding on to him, trembling in case the scrabbling noise should come nearer and she should feel a rat run across the bed.

"Do you think ... there are ... many of ... them?" she whispered.

Her voice was shaking. Over her head the Count saw
a large very thin cat with a long tail silhouetted against
the light as it pushed its way past the side of the bear-
skin into the outer cavern.

He was smiling as he tightened his arms.

"You are quite safe as long as you keep close to
me," he said.

Vesta awoke to find she was alone. She raised her head
but there was no sign of him.

Then she realised it was very much lighter than it
had been the night before. The bear-skin was slightly
drawn aside and she could see people moving in the
outer cave.

She sat up on the soft bed and realised that the
Count was amongst them.

She could see he was shaving with the razor which
she knew he carried in the saddle-bag on his horse, and
there were a number of children standing round
watching him do it.

She rose from the bed and saw in dismay that her
skirt was badly creased. Standing up she tried to shake
it and the petticoats she wore beneath it.

When the Duchess had purchased the green riding-
habit from one of the most expensive habit-makers in
London, she had certainly not anticipated it would
have such rough usage as it was enduring now.

At the end of the bed Vesta saw the bundle of her
small possessions which the Count must have brought
in for her.

She was glad to have her brush and comb and although there was no mirror this morning in which she
could see her reflection, she tidied her hair as best she
could.

'It would be useless,' she thought, 'to ask for water
in which to wash.'

Besides she had the feeling that the one thing the
Count wanted more than anything else, was for them to
get away while they were still free to go.

Picking up her cloak and her bundle, Vesta moved
into the big cave.

At the sight of her instantly there was a rush of women at her side. The mother of the baby came first holding it in her arms, talking excitedly.

Vesta looked at the baby, first apprehensively, and then with delight. There was no doubt the child was better! It was no longer blue in the face and when she touched his tiny hands, they were quite warm.

The mother was obviously explaining that it had had several feeds of goat's milk. Vesta drew her other glove from her pocket.

She saw the Count was near and said to him:

"Explain to this woman that she must keep the gloves carefully and use a new finger only when the old one is useless. If the hole grows too big, the baby will get his milk too quickly and it will give him indigestion."

The Count conveyed the message and the woman nodded to show that she understood.

There were a number of other questions which not only concerned the health of the children.

While the Count was trying to arrange for the horses to be saddled, he kept being fetched back to translate Vesta's remedies for ailments from which apparently the whole community suffered.

Vesta had been thinking of what would help the people.

Now she told the Count that they were to pick garlic and take it in hot milk and honey when anyone suffered from a sore throat or had a cough.

"And gentian is an excellent tonic for women who are anaemic like the mother of this tiny baby," she said. "I saw lots of the blue trumpet flowers on our way up the mountain, but tell them the yellow ones are best."

The Count smiled.

"That is one remedy of which I have heard," he said. "The legend is it was revealed to King Ladislavs of Hungary when he prayed his people might be saved from the plague which was ravaging the country."

Vesta's eyes lit up.

"That is a lovely story," she said. "Tell them to slice the root, add a little wine and take a large spoonful before meals. If they keep it corked in a bottle they can take it all through the winter."

"We have to go," the Count said in a low voice. "Tell them one more way of keeping themselves healthy so that they can go on robbing and killing travellers, and then we must say goodbye!"

"I hope that they cannot understand you," Vesta said hastily.

"It is quite safe," the Count answered. "What do you want me to say?"

"Birch-bark is also a good tonic," Vesta said. "I can see that some of the children have eczema and that will help them as it purifies the blood. And Mama always believed it was good internally for older people."

The Count told the women what she had said, and then firmly ignoring the further stream of questions which kept pouring from their lips, he drew Vesta to the mouth of the cave.

"We have to be blindfolded," he said, "so say goodbye."

Vesta held out her hand to the Chief Brigand's wife whose child she had saved from suffocating. But to her embarrassment the woman went down on her knees and kissed it.

The other women followed until the Count covered Vesta's eyes with his cravat as he had done before, and lifting her up in his arms sat her on her horse.

Then she knew that he too was blindfolded and the men led them forward amid loud cries of farewell from the Chief Brigand.

There was a sudden yell of anguish from the women.

"They say that they will never see you again," the Count translated.

"Tell them that I will come to them," Vesta answered, "or that they shall come to me. Say I promise I will not forget them."

"Are you sure you want me to say that?" the Count asked.

"Quite sure," Vesta replied.

He obviously repeated with some eloquence what she had told him to say because there was a cry of delight, and although she was unable to see the women, she waved her hand and was sure they were waving in reply.

They were calling after her until finally her horse carried her out of ear-shot.

Once again she knew the Count was riding ahead and that she had nothing to do but to follow.

But now instead of riding in silence, the men were talking, joking and laughing and the Count was joining in.

Sometimes he talked to them for a long time and they appeared to listen respectfully.

They rode a long way moving first straight over very rocky ground until they moved a little way down hill.

Finally the Brigands drew the horses to a standstill.

"They are leaving us now," the Count said, "you can take the bandage from your eyes."

Vesta obeyed and she saw they were once again amongst trees on a path very like the one from which they had been taken.

The Count drew some money from his coat-pocket and handed it to the Headman who had been in charge as he had been when they were captured.

He made a gesture as if he would not take it. But the Count obviously insisted and Vesta was sure that he said it was for the women and children.

The men all shook hands with the Count. Then he turned to Vesta and said:

"They wish to pay their homage to you for what you have done for them all. Just sit still, they will not take your hand."

Vesta looked at the men wonderingly. They came round to the side of her horse and each one knelt on one knee and kissed the hem of her habit.

One after another they approached her with their heads down, until the Headman with his squint eye stared at her boldly and she thought with a look of lust in his eyes.

Yet he too knelt and kissed the hem of her habit, and then with a farewell and a wave of the hands, the Brigands swarmed up the side of the mountain under the trees and in a very few seconds were out of sight.

Vesta looked after them and then she asked:

"Why did they . . . kiss my . . . skirt . . . like that?"

"Already they are canonising you," the Count replied. "They have seen you perform two miracles of healing and therefore they regard you as a Saint."

"They must not think . . . that of . . . me," Vesta said. "I am not . . . good enough."

"One woman said to me, 'She is an angel from God' and that is what you looked like in the cave."

Vesta looked at him uncertainly. He must be teasing or mocking at her, she thought, but the expression in his eyes seemed serious and sincere.

The Count drew a deep breath.

"I have been in many dangerous situations in my life," he said, "but never one to equal that! And there is only one person I can thank for rescuing me, and that is you. Do you realise, Ma'am, that you have saved us both?"

"You did not think this morning that they would release us?" Vesta asked.

"I hoped they would," the Count replied. "In their own way they have their principles and standards of honour. But Brigands and robbers, as you can well understand, are not entirely predictable."

There was a smile on his lips as he added:

"As we have been so fortunate—let us get out of here quickly!"

He galvanized his horse into a trot and now they were moving along the path at a greater speed than they had ever moved before.

In a short while the trees thinned out and now they had occasionally a breathtakingly beautiful view of the valley and even at some points so far ahead that Vesta thought that at any moment she must see the spires and towers of Djilas.

After riding for several hours the Count drew in his horse to look ahead and said:

"The Brigands took us some distance out of our way, so I am afraid it is unlikely that we can reach Djilas tonight."

"Is there anywhere we can stay?" Vesta asked apprehensively.

"Yes, there is . . ." he began.

Then even as he spoke Vesta who was gazing into the valley ahead of them gave an exclamation.

"Look! There are men down there!"

Far away in the distance, where the white road wound between high mountains on either side, it was easy with good eyes to see there were a number of men on horse-back on the road, while others on foot were moving across a field.

The Count sat staring without speaking.

"Are they soldiers?" Vesta asked, noticing that something they wore or carried glinted in the sunshine.

"I do not know," the Count answered, "but I suggest we take no chances."

He moved ahead without saying more and Vesta followed him. She wondered if yet another frightening adventure lay in wait for them.

In a very short while, however, the Count rode into a deep ravine in which they were completely hidden and guiding the horses through low scrub started climbing.

Quite unexpectedly they suddenly reached the top and now they started going downhill between trees— not the thick dark firs through which they had ridden the day before.

There were silver birch, juniper, strawberry trees, myrtle, and once again the purple loveliness of the Judas tree.

Down they went until turning a little westwards they came upon a cascade of water pouring down the side of the mountain. It was not very wide but full and silver as it fell straight, then splashed over volcanic stones which sometimes formed a pool.

Now in the warm sunshine Vesta realised that they were once more amongst the flowers and the flowering shrubs.

There were huge bushes of wild rose and thorny smilax. There was gold and yellow broom, azaleas, rhododendrons and dozens of other shrubs she did not recognise, until suddenly the Count led her on to something resembling an Alpine plateau.

Never had she realised flowers could be so glowing, so beautiful, so breath-takingly colourful!

Beside the small plateau the cascade had formed an enormous pool almost like a dam before it flowed over the edge and cascaded once again further down into the valley.

The Count drew his horse to a standstill and waited for Vesta to catch up with him.

"I have the idea," he said, "that I may be able to provide you with luncheon."

"How?" Vesta asked.

She realised as he spoke that she was hungry. There had only been black bread and goat's cheese for breakfast. And she had forced herself to drink some goat's milk although she dared not think of the condition of the cup in which it was brought her.

"I am trying to remember how we caught trout when I was a boy," he said. "We used to come camping in these hills, and unless I have lost the knack I think we will both enjoy a fresh trout for luncheon!"

"Can you really catch one?" Vesta asked.

"I do not wish you to see me fail," the Count answered, "so I suggest you leave your horse here and walk a little way down towards the valley. Do not go out of earshot and be careful of snakes. But if you can find a lemon tree or some oranges they would greatly improve our meal."

"They would indeed," Vesta cried excitedly. "And there should be strawberries too! I will put them in my hat."

She dismounted as she spoke, and taking off her hat which she had hung once again by its ribbons down her back, she held it upside down like a basket.

As the sun was very hot she took off her jacket and flung it down on the grass amongst the flowers.

"You will come if I call?" she asked. "There might be another snake!"

"I shall be listening," the Count assured her.

He too had taken off his coat and was rolling up his sleeves. He had not replaced his cravat when she had drawn it from her eyes.

As if he knew what she was thinking, he said with an amused smile:

"Will you forgive me for not being correctly dressed on this particular occasion?"

Vesta flushed.

"Yes of course!" she said, and added shyly: "I would not like you to think that I was being ... critical, especially after you were so ... kind as to lend me your cravat as a bandage. I could not have borne the rags they carried to have ... touched me!"

She paused and then she said:

"If I seemed prudish when we first met, it was only because I had never seen a ... gentleman with his shirt ... open before."

The Count smiled.

"You are very young," he said softly, "and yet there is so much wisdom in that small golden head."

His tone was caressing and Vesta stared at him wide-eyed, before her eyes dropped before his and she turned and hurried away through the flowers.

She had only to go a short distance before she found a lemon tree. She imagined the Count wanted them for the fish and thought four would be plenty.

She had intended to keep her hat for the strawberries, but sadly she could not find any.

This valley was obviously more sheltered than the one they had passed through before, and the strawberry plants had already shed their fruit.

Instead there were ripe oranges like golden balls and wild raspberries growing in such profusion that Vesta easily filled her hat with them and was forced to carry the oranges and lemons in her arms.

There was no sign of any snakes, and the beauty of the flowering shrubs, the wonder of the flowers at her feet, made her feel she had strayed into some strange Paradise.

'How lovely if I could stay here for ever!' she thought.

Then she need not be afraid of going to Djilas, of meeting the Prince or having to behave in the Royally circumspect manner. That alone had made her feel nervous ever since she had learnt she was to be a Princess.

Then she told herself she was being nonsensical

again. She had to look forward to what lay ahead, she
had to believe that she would be happy in her new life.

She walked slowly back to the plateau to find the
Count had made a fire.

It was burning brightly and Vesta's first thought was
that it would prove very hot until she realised that he
had considerately set it to one side of the plateau,
where the smoke would blow in the opposite direction
from where they would be sitting amongst the flowers.

When she reached him he looked up and smiled.

"Have you had any luck?" she asked.

He pointed to where at the side of the pool there lay
six silver trout.

"You have caught them!" she cried. "How clever of
you!"

"I snatched them," he corrected, "that is, I believe,
the right expression used by all experienced poachers."

He saw the admiration in her eyes and added:

"I must be truthful and admit it was surprisingly
easy! So few people come here that the fish are almost
tame."

Vesta looked into the pool. Numbers of blue mountain trout were darting about in the water. She put
down her fruit saying:

"How are you going to cook them?"

"I have been trying to remember how we did it when
I was young," the Count answered. "With your knowledge of herbs could you find me some wild fennel?"

"But of course," Vesta answered, "there is masses of
it everywhere."

She pointed to the flat-topped golden flowers,
growing to a height of five or six feet amongst the
shrubs.

"There it is," she said. "But I shall need your knife
to cut it. The stalks are tough."

"I will cut it for you," he said. "Just show me which
it is, so I do not make a mistake."

They gathered an armful of fennel and Vesta
watched the Count wrap it round the fish so that they
were completely covered.

"Fennel is supposed to give those who eat it long
life, strength and courage," she smiled.

"What are the herbs for love?" the Count asked.

"I do not think I know them," Vesta answered quickly.

"I think you do," he replied seeing the flush of colour of her white skin.

"The country folk at home believe in Ladies Slipper and Ladies Tresses," she said at length as he was obviously awaiting her answer. "They are wild orchids. All orchids have a . . . reputation for being used in . . . love potions."

"I am sure we have no need of one," he said quietly.

Vesta wondered what he meant.

By this time there was plenty of glowing ash in the heart of the fire and the Count laid the fish in it, one after another.

They argued as to how long the fish would take to be well cooked, and Vesta found that her estimate was right when they undid the first one.

The skin came away easily and the flesh was white right to the bone.

The fish of course were very hot and they laughed as they burnt their fingers. They squeezed the lemons over the pieces they wished to eat and nothing could have been more delicious.

"I have never had a better dish in my li e!" Vesta cried. "You are a far better cook than I am!"

"I think the answer lies in the fact that we are both very hungry," the Count smiled. "It is a long time since we have tasted anything edible!"

"Do not let us remember the goat's meat last night," Vesta pleaded with a little shudder. "It looked so horrible I felt I was being a cannibal even putting it in my mouth."

She laughed.

"I am sure those poor dogs had indigestion all night."

"It was lucky they were there," the Count said. "It would have been considered an insult not to have enjoyed the animal they had specially killed in our honour."

Vesta put the oranges and the raspberries in front of him.

"The strawberries are finished in this valley," she said, "but I think I really prefer raspberries."

"So do I," the Count said.

"Could any picnic be more delectable?" Vesta asked as they finished the fruit, "or any setting more beautiful?"

She stared around her. Then looking at her fingers said:

"I must wash in the pool. Incidentally that is something I might have done before luncheon."

She moved across to the pool and knelt down. She put her arms in up to her elbows and felt the water was icy cold. Yet it was so clean and lovely she wished she could undress and bathe in it.

Then she cupped the water in the palms of her hands and splashed it onto her face.

Only when she was blinded did she remember that her handkerchief was in the pocket of her jacket.

"Please will you bring me my handkerchief?" she called to the Count. "I have left it in my pocket."

"I will get it for you," he answered.

Once again Vesta splashed water against her face and then, as she heard him moving beside her, she held out her hand for the handkerchief.

Her eyes were closed, the drops of water on her cheeks iridescent in the sunshine.

She felt him kneel down beside her and he began to dry her face.

"Thank you," she said putting up one hand to take the handkerchief from him.

Then he pulled her backwards into his arms and before she could realise what was happening, his lips were on hers.

For a moment as she felt the hard pressure of his mouth, she was still from sheer astonishment.

Then as she tried to put out her hands to push him away, something like quick-silver ran through her body—a feeling so wonderful, so ecstatic, she could not move.

She could only feel, as she had never felt before, a rapture that seemed to make her vibrate with an emotion she had not known existed.

The Count's arms were holding her so tightly she could hardly breathe. His mouth, passionate and possessive held her captive and she felt thrill upon thrill ripple through her until she was no longer herself, but part of him.

She felt as if he drew her very heart and took it from her body. Everything that was beautiful and lovely, spiritual and perfect, was suddenly identified with the feeling he evoked in her.

How long he held her she had no idea, but when he raised his head she could only stare up at him, bemused to the point when she only knew that her will and her very identity were no longer her own.

"God, I love you!" he said hoarsely in Katōnian and his voice was unsteady.

Then he was kissing her again, kissing her slowly with deep, fierce, demanding kisses so that she stirred and moved beneath the violence of his lips.

At the same time a flame was flickering within her breast and responding wildly to the fire that burnt in him.

Finally when they seemed to touch the very peaks of the mountains, when she thought the ecstasy within her must lift her into the sky itself, he raised his head once again.

With a little cry and an effort that was almost superhuman, Vesta drew herself from his arms.

She could only move a few feet away from him and then she sank down amongst the flowers, her whole body trembling, her hands going instinctively to her breast.

She stared at him her eyes wide and questioning, her lips quivering from his kisses.

"H-how . . . c-could . . . you?" she asked in a whisper.

"I love you."

His voice was very deep, his dark eyes were on hers.

"But . . . it is . . . wrong," she tried to say.

Then one hand went to her mouth and she murmured almost as if she spoke to herself:

"I-I did not . . . k-know a . . . kiss could be . . . l-like . . . that."

"A kiss is not like that," the Count said, "unless two people truly love each other."

"But we . . . cannot, we . . . must not," Vesta stammered.

"Why not?" the Count asked, "I am a man! And no man, my lovely darling, could be with you as I have been these last two days and not love you."

"I do . . . not . . . understand," she said pathetically.

"Is it so very difficult?" he asked. "You are the most beautiful woman I have ever seen in my life! You are also the bravest, the sweetest, and the kindest! Could one ask more of one small person?"

"You . . . must not . . . say these . . . things," Vesta cried. "It is . . . wrong . . . you know it is . . . wrong!"

"Is love ever wrong?" the Count enquired.

"I do not . . . know about . . . love," Vesta said.

"But I do," he answered, "and real love comes only once in our life. A love which is everything a man and a woman seek, pray for and hope they will one day find."

He saw her quiver and said gently:

"That is the love I have for you."

"I . . . should . . . not . . . listen," Vesta faltered, "I . . . I must go . . . away."

But she did not move and after a moment the Count said:

"When you lay last night in my arms, I knew that you were all I wanted, all I asked for in the whole world."

"I should not have done . . . anything so . . . i-improper," Vesta murmured , "but it was the . . . rats!"

"If it had not been the rats it would have been something else," the Count replied. "I believe we were meant for each other and we would have found each other somehow, sometime, whatever barriers lay between us."

At his words Vesta put her hands up to her face and covered her eyes with her fingers.

"I must . . . not . . . listen," she said. "You . . . know that I am . . . married."

"To a man you have never seen."

"That is not . . . the point," Vesta protested. "I am

... married to ... him ... legally. You must not ... talk to me like ... this. Why ... oh why ... did you ... kiss me?"

"I kissed you because I could not help it," the Count said, "and when my lips touched yours, I felt you respond. You wanted my kiss, my precious, as I want you. Do not lie, tell me that you love me."

"I . . . cannot . . . I must . . . not!" Vesta cried. "Please . . . please do not . . . make me . . . love you!"

It was the cry of a child and the Count looked at her for a long moment before he said very softly:

"It is too late! Your lips, Heart of my Heart, have told me of your love."

Chapter Six

"No! No!" Vesta cried.

Then even as she spoke she knew that what the Count had said was the truth.

She did love him! Her hatred had been transformed into love and she had not been aware of it!

She had indeed hated him at first, because he was so imperious, so aggressively determined, so overwhelmingly masculine. She had hated him, and yet there had been a fascination in feeling so intensely about any man.

He had disturbed her and she had found it impossible not to be increasingly aware of him every moment they were together.

Even though she had tried to immerse herself in her day-dreams as they had ridden through the forest, she had known with a strangely sharp awareness that he was there and that he was encroaching upon her consciousness.

'And now I love him,' she thought wildly.

She knew then that her hatred had turned to love at the moment when, dreaming about him at the Inn, she had awoken to find him staring at her from the other side of the fire-place.

Her dream had been so vivid, so real.

She had been falling from the cliff's edge, and as she fell she was petrified with that shrinking, panic-stricken terror which she always felt when she encountered heights.

She had tried to scream for help but knew that no-one could save her. Until suddenly from out of the sky an eagle had swept towards her!

She had felt the bird's wings enfolding her, holding her secure, saving her from the destruction she feared. Then as she gasped in relief, she had known the eagle was the Count!

Her dream had given her a feeling of security and comfort. It had also brought her another emotion, but she had not realised what it was.

'It was love!' she thought now—a love which had made her trust the Count to kill her rather than be left at the mercy of the Brigands.

Strangely enough she had not felt fear when she waited for his knife.

She had thought afterwards it was because she was numb with terror, but she knew now it was because loving him she was prepared to die at his hand and had known he would not fail her.

'I love him,' she told herself in her heart and knew that only with a man she loved could she have lain all night in his arms and been neither ashamed or afraid.

How could she have been so blind, so stupid as not to recognise love when it came to her?

Then she remembered the ceremony which had taken place in London in front of the Registrar.

At No. 10 Downing Street, with only her father and the Viscount Castlereagh as witnesses, the Prime Minister of Katōna had stood proxy for his Prince and in a few short minutes she had been united in marriage with a man she had never seen.

'But I am in fact married to Prince Alexander,' Vesta thought.

How could she have known or even dreamt that she could feel like this for another man and one she had known only for two days?

She drew in her breath, one hand still against her heart as if she would quell its beating, and realised that the Count was watching her.

There was a burning fire in his dark eyes and after one glance at him she looked away towards the cascade.

She looked ethereal and very lovely. The sun turned her fair hair to spun gold, the flowers framed her like a garland, the column of her neck rose white and round above the thin muslin of her blouse.

"You are so beautiful!" the Count said hoarsely. "I did not realise there was so much loveliness in the world."

Vesta did not answer. After a moment he said, his voice deepening:

"Do you know what I would like to do?"

She shook her head, finding it difficult to speak.

"I would like to carry you away to a cave in the mountains where we would be alone," he said, "and there I would compel you to tell me that you loved me. I would kiss you, beat you, even torture you, until I knew that you were really mine—as you were always meant to be."

His voice seemed to vibrate on the air as he went on.

"I would possess not only your soft lips and your wonderful desirable body, but also your thoughts, your feelings, the very breath you draw. I want every scrap of you, Vesta, I want you—the whole of you and for ever."

His words made a quiver run through her. He saw the breath come quicker between her lips as he continued:

"You say you do not know about love. Let me tell you what love means, not to the pale-blooded English who think it vulgar to show emotion, but to me and to men like me who live in this country."

Again there was a note in his voice to which Vesta could not help feeling herself respond. But she forced herself not to look up at him.

"Love—real love such as I have for you," the Count said, "is like a forest fire, all consuming, destructive, so violent so that there is no controlling it. Love is also like a tempest at sea, tumultuous and overpowering, ready to destroy those who challenge its supremacy."

He paused, then his voice rang out:

"It is a force, a power, it triumphs and it conquers! That is love, Vesta! How can anyone as small as you resist it or withstand it?"

Still she did not answer, and now the Count's voice changed and he said softly:

"Love is also the sunshine, the song of the birds, the sound of the bees, the flowers at your feet. That too is love, my sweet darling. Because it is a part of us, around us and within us, there is no escape."

"But we ... c-cannot ... we must ... not," Vesta tried to say.

"Who can stop love?" the Count asked. "Not all the words mumbled over you in London by some legal dignitary, not all the signatures on pieces of paper, not all the Statesmen in Europe can prevent us at this moment from loving each other."

She did not answer.

"Look at me!"

She trembled but she did not turn her head.

"Look at me, Vesta," he said commandingly.

Very slowly, her eyes wide and afraid, she turned her face towards him.

For a long moment they looked at each other. Vesta felt as if some force was pressing her towards him. She was being propelled by a power so strong, so irresistible, that it moved her physically.

She felt herself tremble, she felt her whole being reach out towards him and she wanted, because she was afraid, the security and safety of his arms.

Then when it seemed as if it was impossible for her not to touch him and raise her lips to his, she gave a little cry and put her hands up to her face.

"I want you," he said, "you are mine, Vesta!"

"No ..." she murmured against her hands, "no ... no!"

He looked at her for a long moment before he rose to his feet. He walked a few steps away from her to stand looking down into the sunlit pool from which he had taken the trout.

Then in a strange voice, harsh and discordant, he said:

"So a crown does mean more to a woman than love! You love me, but rather than admit it you will go on to Djilas because there you will take your place as a Princess and that is more important to you than anything else. I hope you find the plaudits of the crowd an adequate compensation for my kisses."

His voice was so bitter that Vesta felt as if he had struck her, and she winced from the pain of it. Then she said, her words fumbling over one another:

"How could you ... think such a ... thing of ... me? How could you believe that it is for that ... reason I am marrying ... the Prince?"

"What do you expect me to think?" the Count asked without turning.

"Please," Vesta pleaded, "please ... let me ... explain to ... you."

"What is there to explain?" he asked roughly. "You have made your decision. As you told me when we first met—your place is with your husband."

Vesta rose and moved towards him, her face very pale. When she reached his side she said:

"May I tell you ... why I ... accepted ... Prince Alexander's ... offer of ... marriage?"

"I am sure you have a very adequate explanation," the Count answered, and now he was sneering.

"Please ... listen to ... me," Vesta pleaded.

"If it pleases you," he said sullenly.

"Can we sit in the ... shade of the trees?" Vesta asked. "The sun is very ... hot."

"Of course," he said in tones of conventional courtesy, "I should have thought of it before."

She looked up at him beseechingly.

His face was set in hard lines and once again he looked like an eagle, ruthless, detached and somehow inhuman.

She gave a little sigh that was almost a sob and walked away from the sunshine into the shadow of the silver birch trees.

There was moss at their roots and Vesta sat down, smoothing her full green skirt into some semblance of tidiness.

The Count did not sit but leant against the trunk of an adjacent tree.

She felt that he had deliberately withdrawn himself from her and that he despised her. She dared not look at his face because she was afraid of the contempt she would see in his eyes.

"I told you," she began in a low voice, "that I do not

know about ... love, and that is true. I have never
been in love. But I have always felt that one day I
should find a man that I could ... love and then ...
we would be ... married."

She had spoken hesitatingly and now her voice
seemed to falter away into silence. She felt that a great
gulf yawned between herself and the Count.

He was making no effort to understand. She was
alone and separated from him as she had not been
since they first met.

"Please ... please," she begged, "try to understand
what I am ... trying to tell you. It is so ... difficult,
but I want you to ... know."

"I am listening," he said.

"Will you not sit down?" she asked. "You are so tall
and I feel ... you are ... far away."

"Why do you feel that?"

"I do not know. I just ... feel that you have ... left
me."

"Does that make you feel insecure and lonely?"

"You ... know it ... does."

His eyes searched her face. Then he sat down almost
opposite her, his back against another tree trunk.

He was still withdrawn and yet she found it not so
difficult as it had been to continue speaking.

"I have always wanted to love ... someone," Vesta
went on, "because I was not loved as a child as I ...
might have been."

"What do you mean by that?" the Count asked.

"Papa always wanted a son," Vesta answered. "The
Salfonts are a very old family. There were Earls of Salfont in the 13th Century, and when our ancestor was
given a Dukedom after fighting with Marlborough, it
was only another chapter in the long history of how
well the Salfonts served the crown and England."

There was a touch of pride in her voice before she
went on:

"We were all brought up to believe we had a great
responsibility towards our country and its people."

"I have heard of your family," the Count said.

"Then you will understand," Vesta continued, "how
important it was for Papa to have a son. But he and

Mama had five daughters before Gerald was born. Mama has often said to me:

"'I prayed, Vesta, I prayed every night that I could give your father the son he wanted so desperately. When each baby was born, the first question I always asked was—

'What is it?' And the midwife would reply: 'I am sorry, Your Grace, another daughter.'"

There was a little throb in Vesta's voice.

She loved her mother and it never ceased to hurt her that she herself had brought her parents so much disappointment.

"After Gerald was born," she went on, "the doctor said that Mama should not have any more children. But she and Papa were so anxious to have a second son, just as a safeguard in case anything ... happened to the first."

Vesta paused for a moment. She glanced at the Count and realised he did not look so contemptuous and her voice was a little stronger as she continued:

"But instead of another boy, I arrived! After that the doctors said very firmly that it would kill Mama to have any more children."

"So you were unwanted," the Count said.

"Papa and Mama were always very kind to me," Vesta said, "but I soon knew how deeply disappointed they were and how happy it would have made them if I had been a boy."

She looked away towards the sunshine and the falling cascade.

"That knowledge coloured my whole childhood," she said. "Perhaps that is why I sought escape in day-dreams for which I often used to be punished. I suppose I was afraid to face reality."

"As you are now," the Count interposed quietly.

"And when Gerald was killed at Waterloo," Vesta went on, "I felt ashamed of being ... me."

"So he died at Waterloo?" the Count said.

"I thought it would kill Papa," Vesta said. "For a long time we dared not speak of Gerald in his presence. Then gradually he became more like his original self, but there was a sadness about him that had never been there before."

"Surely there is an heir to the Dukedom?" the Count asked.

"Of course," Vesta answered, "Papa's brother's son. We have never liked him, and sometimes I think Papa even hates Rupert, which is understandable."

She paused, as if she was thinking what she should say next and then she said hesitantly:

"You may think I am a . . . long time coming to the . . . point in this . . . story, but I wanted you to . . . understand why I came to Katōna."

"Go on," the Count said.

"When Papa told me that your Prince had asked for my hand in marriage, I was completely astonished. I could not believe that he would expect me to do anything so unexpected, so terrifying, as to accept such an offer.

" 'But I do not know the Prince!' I cried.

"Then Papa explained to me that Royal marriages are arranged, that it was not really the Prince who had asked for me but his Government."

"Did that make much difference?" the Count asked.

"It did to . . . me," Vesta answered. "I told Papa that I could not contemplate for a moment marrying at the request of a Government, or for that matter marrying a man I had never seen and about whom I knew nothing."

As she spoke she could see herself in the library at Salfont House looking out onto the trees in Berkeley Square and trying to visualise a strange country called Katōna which apparently wished her to rule over it.

"Katōna has always been very friendly with Great Britain," her father had said, "and it is important that they should remain so."

He was standing with his back to the fireplace as he spoke and Vesta felt herself shiver, not from the cold of the room but because there was an inflexible note in her father's voice which she recognised.

He has always been rather a martinet where his daughters were concerned. At the same time he had never forced any of them into marriage with a man for whom she had no liking.

When the Marquis of Severn had proposed to Harriet and she had said that she could not contemplate becoming his wife, the Duke had not tried to press her.

Although he was disappointed he had allowed her instead to marry a mere baronet to whom she had irretrievably given her heart.

"I am sorry, Papa," Vesta said. "While I am deeply ... honoured by the suggestion that I should marry Prince Alexander, the answer is of course ... no."

"Why 'of course'?" the Duke enquired.

"Because I have no wish to marry without love," Vesta replied. "You and Mama have always been happy together, and my sisters are happy too. Caroline said to me only last week that she and Robert were more in love with each other now than when they first married."

"This is different," the Duke said slowly.

"Why is it different, Papa?" Vesta enquired.

"Because in marrying Prince Alexander you would be doing a service to your country," he answered.

He had walked across the room as he spoke to stand staring up at a picture which hung on the wall.

It was a picture of his son Gerald, painted when he first joined the Grenadier Guards. It was a good likeness.

The Prince Regent's favourite portrait painter, Lawrence, had caught the sparkle in his eye, the smile on his lips, the youthful enthusiasm which had caused him to be loved wherever he went.

"I am willing to do ... many things for England," Vesta said nervously, as if she already knew what was coming, "but not to spend the rest of my life away from you all in a strange country with a man whom I do not know and who does not know me."

There had been silence in the library and then her father had said quietly:

"Gerald gave his life for England, Vesta. All I am asking you to do is to serve your country as you would have been willing to do had you been a boy. You cannot fight for England as Gerald did, but in this way you can serve her as the Salfonts have done all down the centuries."

The Duke's voice had been full of pain.

Once again Vesta realised how the loss of his son was still as agonising as it had been when the news had first arrived that Gerald had been killed in battle.

She had wanted to go on protesting, she had known that every nerve in her body was rebelling against such a sacrifice, against a decision which was contrary to her deepest instincts.

Then as she opened her lips to speak, to tell her father that it was impossible, that she would do anything else, anything except marry the ruler of Katōna, she had seen the tears in his eyes.

There is always for children something horrifying in seeing their parents cry and realising they are not the exalted adults they had thought them to be, but human beings who can suffer.

The Duke had not wept when he had learnt that Gerald had been killed. He had remained stony-faced when a memorial to his son was dedicated in the parish church beside the vault which held a number of their ancestors.

He had not cried when the Duke of Wellington himself had told him of Gerald's bravery in the battle and how he had rallied his men again and again against the French, until finally he died from a bullet in the heart.

Yet now there were tears in the Duke's eyes.

"Papa was ... crying," Vesta told the Count in a whisper.

"I knew then," she went on, "there was nothing I could do but accept the offer of marriage from Katōna."

She wiped away a tear, before she asked:

"How could I tell Papa I was a ... coward. As you know I am frightened of so ... many things, but I was more frightened at that moment of ... hurting him."

Her voice died away and now she looked towards the Count with an appeal in her eyes as if she begged him to understand.

"It is one thing to die in battle in the heat of the engagement," the Count said slowly. "There is an exhilaration in fighting which I think carries a man into the arms of death without fear. But this is different."

He looked at Vesta as he said quietly:

"Can you really contemplate living day after day, month after month, year after year with a man you may not like, with a man who may repel you?"

He saw Vesta clasp her hands together, and he went on:

"Only the English could think of making a demand so inhuman, so cruel on someone as sensitive as you. Just as they send their precious sons away to boarding schools where they are beaten or starved, so your father was prepared to send you to a strange country of which you knew nothing, to marry a man you had never even seen."

"Lord Castlereagh said . . . the Prince . . . was intelligent and a . . . good sportsman," Vesta faltered.

"And what else did you learn about him?" the Count asked.

Vesta was silent and he said:

"I have the feeling you have heard something more. Tell me."

Still she did not speak and he said again:

"Tell me what you heard!"

It was a command and Vesta replied hesitantly:

"I . . . I did not mean to . . . listen. It was when we were at sea . . . the Prime Minister, the Captain and the Aide-de-camp were . . . talking in the Saloon . . . I was hanging up my cloak . . . in the corridor. It had got wet on deck."

"And what did you hear?" the Count asked.

"They were . . . talking about . . . the Prince and . . . me."

"What did they say?"

Vesta's voice was very low as she answered:

"The Aide-de-camp said I was too . . . unsophisticated to be able to . . . cope with what . . . lay ahead."

"Did the Prime Minister agree?"

Vesta did not answer and the Count said:

"I want to know."

"They said," Vesta said slowly, "that the Prince had a . . . fondness for . . . someone . . . else . . ."

"And it upset you?" the Count asked.

"I had not . . . imagined there would be . . . anyone like . . . that," Vesta said. "Perhaps that is . . . why they . . . thought I was . . . unsophisticated."

"You thought that when you came to Katōna," the Count said in his deep voice, "the Prince would be waiting, that you would fall in love with each other and live happily ever after! Is that the truth?"

"I . . . hoped we . . . m-might be . . . f-friends," Vesta stammered.

"Friends?" the Count questioned. "Why should you expect friendship in marriage?"

"I thought I . . . might help His Royal Highness . . . with the people," Vesta said, "that is why I studied Katōna on the voyage . . . why I tried to . . . learn from the Aide-de-camp and the Prime Minister about the country and its . . . people."

"And did you ask them about the Prince himself?"

"No . . . no!"

"Why not?"

"I felt . . . shy at appearing . . . inquisitive."

"And yet that was surely the most important thing for you to know!" the Count said. "Instead of which you made an image in your mind of what you wanted the Prince to be. A paper Prince, not a human being, but a man who was a part of your dreams."

Vesta drew in a deep breath before she asked almost pathetically:

"What . . . else could . . . I do?"

"What you can do now is face reality," the Count retorted. "You are in love, little Vesta, the Sleeping Beauty has been awakened by a kiss. My kiss, from my lips."

"But . . . it is . . . wrong."

"It may seem wrong to you," the Count answered. "But what you are intending to do is far more wrong! Do you really imagine you can keep up this farce, this sacrifice forced upon you by your father for the rest of your life? Do you believe that you can act a part so skilfully that it would not be a mockery of what a wife should be?"

She looked at him wide-eyed and he said:

"Wake up, my beloved, you know now you have a fire of your name-sake flickering within you. Feebly at the moment—but it is there and soon it will become an all-consuming blaze from which you cannot escape."

His voice was deep with passion as he said:

"I will teach you about love, Vesta, I will teach you to love me as I love you. I will awaken you to the wonder and glory of it. I will make you live! All I ask in return is that you should tell me of your love for me."

"How can I?" Vesta asked. "I have . . . tried to make you . . . understand why I must . . . go to the . . . Prince, why . . . already I . . . belong to him."

"You belong to me!" the Count contradicted. "Do you imagine for one moment when you kiss the Prince you will respond to his lips as you have responded to mine?"

He saw an involuntary little shiver run through her.

"You have never been kissed before, and when I kissed you just now you said that you did not know a kiss would be like that. I told you then and I tell you again a kiss is not like that save when two people love each other."

His voice softened as he went on:

"A kiss can be all the wonder of the divine, the perfection of a man and woman united because they were meant by God to be one. Or it can be something lewd and beastly."

Again Vesta shivered and now she turned her face away from him so that he could only see her in profile.

Her straight little nose and her sensitive lips were silhouetted against the sunshine and the silver cascade.

"And marriage entails not only a kiss," the Count said relentlessly. "You are very young and very innocent, my Dearest Heart. Have you any idea what happens when a man and a woman are joined together and become, as the Church puts it in the marriage service 'one flesh'?"

"I-I am . . . not . . . c-certain."

"But you can imagine it is something very intimate, something very close, very private. And once again it can be all the wonder and ecstasy of the divine, or something so obscenely degrading that it could frighten you, little Goddess, as you have never been frightened before."

"Other women have ... married without ... love," Vesta said hesitantly.

"A great number of women have done so and are doing so at this moment all over the world," the Count agreed. "Marriages are arranged in England as they are in France and very often in this country. But it usually occurs when the girl is so young that she has not fallen in love with anyone else."

He watched the flicker of Vesta's eyelashes and continued:

"She therefore does not know what to expect from marriage. But, because women are the same the world over, she hopes as you hope, that the Prince of her heart whatever his position in life will awaken her with a kiss!"

He paused, then added:

"But when one has known love already, then it is different."

As he spoke the Count reached out and took Vesta's hand in his.

She felt the hard strength of his fingers and a quiver of delight ran through her.

It was so entrancing, so unexpected, and yet so wonderful that without meaning to do so her small fingers tightened on his, and her eyes lit with sudden radiance.

He looked into her face and smiled.

"You thrill at my touch, my precious one. You are excited because I am near you, because you know I love you and because you cannot help responding to that love."

As if she suddenly remembered what they had been arguing about, Vesta looked away from him. But she did not relinquish her hold on his hand and after a moment he raised her fingers to his lips and kissed them one by one.

Again she felt thrill after thrill run through her. She knew then that she longed, as she had never longed for anything in her whole life, for him to kiss her again on the mouth.

"Which is it to be?" he asked. "The paper Prince?

Or are you prepared to wake up, my Sleeping Beauty, and face life as it is? Are you ready to come really alive and admit that you love me?"

The beguiling note in his voice was almost irresistible. Then he felt her stiffen.

"What is your answer?" he asked.

"When the Prime Minister and the Captain were ... talking in the ship," Vesta answered, "they spoke of ... Madame Züleyha with whom the Aide-de-camp said His Royal Highness was ... besotted. They said she was evil. If she is evil ... must not I try to be ... good?"

The Count released Vesta's hand.

"Madame Züleyha is evil," he said, "and the Prince allowed her to get so much power into her hands that she caused the Revolution."

Vesta's eyes widened.

"You mean it was her fault?" she asked.

"It was his fault," the Count said. "The Prince is weak, Vesta, a weak man who has put his own desires and his own wishes before the needs and the well-being of his country. That is the man to whom you are trying to be loyal!"

His tone was harsh as he continued:

"A man who deliberately, for years, has ignored the wishes of his people, who shut his eyes to the fact that this woman was intriguing against the State and against himself!"

"But what will happen now?" Vesta asked.

"If the Revolutionaries have taken over," the Count said, "then there is every chance that the Turks will try to conquer us. But I am sure that can be avoided. I am not concerned with the politics of Katōna at the moment, Vesta, but of your part in them."

"Do you ... think," Vesta asked in a whisper, "that the Prince will ... refuse to give up ... Madame Züleyha?"

"I think that after what has happened he will have little choice in the matter," the Count answered. "But can you put your faith in him now that you know the truth about him? That is the question you have to ask yourself."

He watched the expression on her face.

"You see, my little goddess of fire, it is not the Prince who has awoken you from your sleep, but I."

Vesta made a little gesture with her hand as he continued:

"However much you may deny it, I know that if I take you in my arms this moment your lips will cling to mine and you will feel again that wonder and rapture which we both knew just now. The whole world will be forgotten because we are close to each other."

His voice once again made Vesta vibrate with an ecstasy which seemed to tingle in her veins and made it hard for her to breathe.

Then as he bent her head so that he could not see the yearning in her eyes or guess how desperately she wanted his kiss, the Count said quietly:

"We have not yet reached Djilas, and we shall not get there tonight. You have twenty four hours, my sweet, in which to make your choice."

"A choice?" she questioned.

"Whether to admit that you belong to me as the gods have intended," he answered, "or whether you must proceed with this senseless self-sacrifice, and go to your paper Prince to become a paper Princess."

She did not move or answer and after a moment he said:

"I want you, dear God! How I want you! As I have never wanted a woman before! I love you, Vesta. I love you—you have taken my heart and soul from me and they are no longer in my keeping, but in yours."

He drew a deep breath.

"You may go to Djilas to help a weak Prince, to support a crumbling régime, to please a cheering crowd. But if you do this you will have destroyed me."

Vesta's head came up quickly and she looked at him enquiringly.

"I mean that," he said in his deep voice. "When a man loves as I love you, that love takes everything else from him. If I cannot have you, if you send me away, I shall then be only the empty shell of what I am now. I love you, I worship you, and I cannot go on through life without you!"

His voice seemed to ring out. Then before Vesta could answer he rose to his feet and bending down helped her to hers.

"We are going on now," he said. "You have twenty four hours in which you can tell me that you love me. If I fail and you go to Djilas without me, I cannot for a moment contemplate the darkness in which I shall be left."

Vesta stood in the shadows of the trees looking up at him.

If she had been in England she knew she would have doubted if what the Count said was the truth, if he could really feel so intensely. But there was no question of the raw sincerity of his voice or the dark yearning in his eyes.

Then as he looked down into her small face, white and frightened, he said softly:

"You are all the beauty of the world, you are all I ask of life and all I hope of Heaven."

His words brought the tears to Vesta's eyes.

But because she was shy, because she was pulsating with so many conflicting emotions which she could not understand, because she wanted to hide her head against his shoulder, she turned and ran away from him.

She ran to where the horses were contentedly cropping the grass on the other side of the plateau, and reaching her horse she leant against the saddle.

'What shall I . . . do?' she whispered in her heart. 'Oh God . . . tell me what I am to . . . do!'

Chapter Seven

Vesta heard the Count approaching her, but she did not turn round. He came nearer until he stood just behind her.

"I have brought your jacket and hat," he said in a quiet voice. "Turn round."

She hesitated before she did as he asked.

He laid her jacket down on the horse's back, set her wide-brimmed hat on her golden hair and tied the ribbons under her chin.

"I do not want you to spoil the perfection of your skin," he said.

He put his fingers under her chin and turned her face up to his.

She thought he was about to kiss her, but instead he said:

"You are so beautiful—so incredibly, heart-breakingly beautiful."

Their eyes met and for a moment neither of them could move. Some magic held them spell-bound as if they looked deeper and deeper into each other's souls.

The Count took his hand away and said hoarsely:

"If you look at me like that, I shall carry you away to that lonely cave and then there will be no decision for you to make now or ever."

He picked her up in his arms and set her on the saddle, put the reins in her hand and arranged her full green skirts as if she was a child.

"I will carry your jacket for you," he said, "but if you feel cold tell me at once. Remember the air from the snows can be treacherous to those who are not used to it."

His concern for her and the gentleness with which he spoke made the tears prick Vesta's eyes.

He thrilled her when he was passionate and commanding. But when he was tender and gentle she felt as if he drew her heart from her body, and she loved him in a way which she could not describe even to herself.

"He is so wonderful," she whispered.

He swung himself into the saddle on his own horse and leaving the plateau behind found a narrow path, little more than a sheep track, leading onwards across the lower part of the mountain.

It was still very warm, but as they proceeded there was a faint breeze in the branches of the trees which fanned Vesta's cheeks and relieved the worst of the heat.

It was difficult however to think of anything but the Count and her love for him.

He had given her twenty-four hours in which to make up her mind and it seemed to her as if she was faced with a dilemma that was worse than walking on the knife-edge of a precipice.

How could she give him up? How could she leave a man who stirred her to the very depths of her being, who aroused in her an ecstasy such as she had never imagined?

On the other hand there was her duty and the promise that she had given not only to her father but to the Registrar in front of the Prime Minister of Katōna and the Viscount Castlereagh that she would marry Prince Alexander.

How could she be so false, so despicable as to refuse to honour her word, to run away from her obligations and responsibilities?

"If only there were someone I could ask to help me decide," she sighed.

She watched the broad shoulders of the Count riding ahead of her.

Every so often he looked back to see that she was still there. She saw the smile on his lips and it was easy to imagine the fire that lay behind his dark eyes.

'Could love really come so swiftly, so overwhelmingly?' Vesta asked herself.

The answer was that she could not question her love. It was there strong and undeniable. And how could she doubt that the Count felt the same wonder and rapture that was hers.

Then with horror she remembered what he had said about Madame Züleyha and the Prince's weakness of character.

Could it be really true that the Prince had protected a woman who was striving to destroy his own country, who could even cause a revolution?

It must have been Madame Züleyha who had wished to send her back to England.

It must have been at her instigation that the Revolutionaries were proceeding to Jēno to compel her to return home on the ship in which she had arrived or, if that was impossible, to destroy her.

Vesta drew in her breath. There were so many dangers in this land!

So many frightening incidents had happened to her since she had arrived, she could hardly believe they were not all a figment of her imagination!

Who would have thought when she left England to become the bride of a Royal Prince, escorted by a Prime Minister and carrying with her an elaborate and expensive trousseau, that she would find herself possessing nothing but what she wore?

But here she was riding with a man she had never seen until three days before and so wildly in love with him that she wanted nothing from life except to be in his arms?

Even to think of the Count, to watch the carriage of his head as he rode in front of her, was enough to make her thrill and tremble as she had done when he touched her.

Then she could see the face of her father, almost like an avenging angel, speaking to her of her duty and the manner in which she could serve her country.

She knew that if he were with her now, there would be no question in his mind as to which course she must take.

He would tell her that she must honour her promise to the Prince, and that, whatever she might learn about him, she had in fact already taken him for better or for worse.

Those were the words in the marriage service which they would repeat to each other when she reached Djilas and they were married in the Cathedral.

For a moment Vesta visualised herself standing at the Altar steps, wearing the white dress which she and her mother had chosen with such care.

"Wonderful jewels will be waiting for you in Katōna," the Duchess had said. "The Prime Minister tells me that the tiara worn by the Princess is almost like a crown, and although I would have liked to send you with the veil that all your sisters have worn when they married, I hear there is a veil that is used there by every Royal bride."

Even then Vesta had found it hard to be really interested in the jewels or anything else she would find in Katōna.

Her thoughts were on the Prince.

She wondered whether he would think her beautiful, whether he would admire the clothes she and her mother had chosen so painstakingly from all the best dress-makers in London, whether they would have much in common.

"And now," she told herself, "clothes and jewels have no importance whatsoever!"

The Count had seen her in only two dresses—the muslin she had worn when she first arrived and he had been so incensed with her, and the green riding-skirt which was creased and dusty from the hard treatment it had received these past two days.

Yet he thought her beautiful!

"Incredibly, heart-breakingly beautiful," he had said, and she felt again the thrill that had run through her at his words.

"What shall I do? What shall I do?"

The words seemed to repeat themselves over and over in her mind to the sound of the horses' hooves moving along the narrow sheep track.

She knew it was a tug-of-war between her brain and her heart.

Her brain told her that she must behave honourably, she must do what was expected of her, that she had come to Katōna as the wife of the Prince and there was no possible escape from what lay ahead.

But her heart cried out with an agony that was like a physical wound. She loved the Count!

"I love him ... I love him!" she said to herself and once again saw her father's face.

She knew the Duke would be utterly ashamed of her should she fail both him and the Prince.

She thought of her mother. Once some years ago, she had listened to her mother talking to her sister, Angeline, before she married.

"You must look after your husband, Angeline," the Duchess had said in her gentle voice.

"Hugo says he is going to look after me," she said.

The Duchess smiled.

"Men always say that when they are in love," the Duchess said. "But when you are married you will find that a woman has to protect, sustain and inspire her husband. That is her job as a wife."

"But how can I protect Hugo?" Angeline asked in surprise.

"You will protect him," the Duchess answered, "from many worries and troubles that you know would upset him. You will protect him from over-exerting himself, from being perturbed by problems about your children, even from being bored by people he dislikes."

The Duchess gave a little laugh.

"If you only knew how often I have protected your father! But of course he has no idea of it."

"I think I understand what you mean, Mama," Angeline said slowly. "But how do I 'sustain' Hugo?"

The Duchess took her daughter's hand in hers.

"You will sustain him, dearest child, when things go wrong," she replied. "If he has financial anxieties, you will help him to realise they are of little importance. You will keep him always believing that things will get better in the future and if, by any chance, he loses someone he loves, he will turn to you in his sorrow and only you can help him."

There was a little break in the Duchess's voice, and Vesta knew she was thinking of Gerald who had been killed.

It was true, she thought, that it was her mother who had been able to help her father in his darkest hour. She had in fact prevented him from breaking down completely when they learnt of Gerald's death.

Yes, the Duchess had certainly sustained her husband in his hour of need. Vesta had wondered then whether she would be able to sustain a man in the same way.

"And lastly you must inspire your husband," the Duchess had continued. "Men need inspiration of women. They do their best, they achieve the impossible, when they are struggling and striving not for themselves but for the woman they love."

She sighed before she continued.

"It is not always easy, Angeline, in fact it is often very difficult. But if you understand what your task entails, if you love the man to whom you are married, then nothing is too difficult, nothing is impossible."

Angeline had listened wide-eyed, and Vesta had wondered if her mother would say the same thing to her when she got married. But her advice to Vesta had been very different.

"You must remember, dear child," she said, "that you will find in marrying a foreigner many difficulties and many problems that you would not have encountered otherwise. Never be critical of your husband even to yourself, and remember that sympathy and understanding are essential for a happy marriage."

Thinking of her words now, Vesta asked herself:

'Am I expected to be sympathetic and understanding about the Prince's infatuation for Madame Züleyha? How can I be? Will we ever be able to discuss such things frankly between us?'

Then she wondered if the Prince loved Madame Züleyha as she loved the Count.

If he did, could their marriage be anything but a hopeless failure from the very beginning?

With each of them yearning for someone else, how intolerable it would be to be forced into a position of pretending publicly that they were happy, of deceiving the people over whom they ruled.

Then almost like a dagger in her heart, Vesta thought of the Count's words when he had said:

"Have you any idea what happens when a man and a woman are joined together?"

She felt a fear of the unknown ripple through her, and she remembered he had gone on to say:

"It can be all the wonders and ecstasy of the divine or something obscenely degrading."

'It will be degrading,' Vesta thought passionately, 'if the Prince loves Madame Züleyha and I love the Count!'

How could they be man and wife, "one flesh", as the marriage service put it, when their marriage was entirely of political necessity and they had no real interest or affection for each other.

'Why, oh, why did I not think of this before I left England?' Vesta asked and knew the answer was very simple: that then she had not been in love!

The horses were moving higher up the hillside and Vesta realised that they would soon be crossing the crest onto the side of the mountains which looked towards Djilas.

The Prince would be waiting for her, and now she found herself thinking of him not as a Prince but as a man.

A man who would kiss her because it was his duty to do so, a man who would be prepared to give her children because they were necessary for the continuance of the Royal House.

'I cannot . . . bear it . . . I cannot!'

Vesta almost cried the words aloud.

Then she remembered the Brigands going down on one knee beside her horse to kiss the hem of her riding-skirt.

They were paying her homage because she had helped them. Would they have done so if they had known she was not a good woman, but one who turned her back on her obligations and her responsibilities?

'If only there was . . . someone who would . . . help me,' Vesta longed again.

And she knew that she yearned beyond everything else to feel the security of the Count's arms around her . . . an eagle protecting her!

She looked ahead and saw that they had reached the summit. The Count had drawn his horse to a standstill and was waiting for her. She hurried her own animal on, eager to be beside him, longing to hear his voice.

"Are you tired, my darling?" he asked as she drew in her horse.

"A little," she answered.

"Then you will be glad to know we have almost no further to go."

Surprised at his words, but realising he was looking below and a little to the left of them, she followed the direction of his eyes.

To her astonishment she saw a house. It was not more than half a mile away, set high on the hillside surrounded by trees on three sides. From where they stood above it she could see it very clearly.

It was built of white stone and its turrets and twisted chimneys gave it a romantic, almost gay appearance.

"A house!" she exclaimed. "Who lives there?"

"It is one of the Royal Hunting Lodges," the Count answered. "The Prince, or any of his courtiers like myself, stay here when we are hunting or shooting in the forests."

He anticipated the question that Vesta was about to ask him by saying:

"Djilas is still three hours' ride from here. I told you that the Brigands took us many miles out of our way."

Vesta looked across the valley as if she expected to see Djilas in the distance. Then she looked back at the house again.

"Can we stay . . . here?" she asked.

"That is what I intend to do," the Count answered. "As a matter of fact I remember that when I was here in March the old couple who had been here for many years were retiring. But they will have been replaced. I think what we both need is a bath and a really civilised meal."

"I enjoyed our luncheon," Vesta said with a smile.

"So did I," he answered.

She knew from the tone of his voice that he was not thinking of the trout they had eaten, but of the moment when he had kissed her.

She flushed a little and they descended the hill towards the house.

As they grew nearer Vesta could see that it was very lovely. Outside the shining windows there was a terrace with a stone balustrade, and below it dropping a little down the hillside there was a cultivated garden with a fountain playing in the centre of it.

Everywhere there were Azaleas, yellow and flame, flanked with shrubs of pink, white and purple blossom.

It was so beautiful that Vesta felt it must be a fairy-tale castle, and her eyes were shining as she turned to the Count and said:

"It is lovely! I would adore to live in a house like this."

"As I have already told you," the Count replied, "it belongs to the Prince."

The thought made her shiver, and now the house did not seem as attractive as before.

The door was at the back and they rode up a short drive and drew their horses to a standstill outside a heavy wooden door reinforced with iron studs.

It had a porch which carried the Royal coat-of-arms which Vesta glanced at a little apprehensively before the Count dismounted and pulled a long chain which hung outside the door.

It was only a few moments before the door opened and a middle-aged man in native dress stood there.

Vesta heard the Count explain who he was and instantly the door was opened wide. Leaving their horses they entered a small hallway.

"I will send a groom, Honourable Bán, for the horses," the servant said.

"They will not wander away," the Count answered, "and see that they are well attended to."

"It shall be done, Honourable Bán."

As the man spoke a woman appeared who Vesta guessed must be his wife, followed by a young girl.

They were both dressed in native costume, a black velvet bodice over a puffed white blouse, a full red skirt and white apron edged with lace.

They curtseyed to Vesta and the Count, who asked their names and then explained that baths were needed as quickly as possible and afterwards a good dinner.

Vesta found the servants were a little difficult to understand, but there was no difficulty in recognising the smiles on their faces or their willingness to please.

The women led Vesta upstairs, showed her into an attractive bed-room which overlooked the front of the house, and told her they would arrange a bath.

While she was waiting she pulled off her hat and walked to the window to look out on the garden and beyond it the beautiful view into the valley.

There was a small lake not far away and the land was thickly wooded.

Then Vesta turned from the window and crossing to the bed lay down on it while she waited for the servants to bring in the bath.

She felt tired and at the same time excited. The reason for her excitement she knew was the realisation that she had one more night alone with the Count.

She had half been afraid as they rode away from the Brigands that they might reach Djilas that night. When he had told her that she had twenty-four hours to make up her mind, it was a reprieve from her own fear of reaching the Palace.

'We shall be alone . . . we can talk together,' she thought and knew it was something wonderful to look forward to, especially as she had never before dined alone with a man.

They had been alone in the Inn that first night. But that could hardly be counted as a proper dinner when she had cooked it herself, and had been too busy hating the Count to realise it marked an important milestone in her life.

But tonight they would be together in civilised surroundings!

Vesta drew in her breath at the thought of it and wondered, though she knew she should not do so, whether he would kiss her.

She shut her eyes and lived again that moment at the side of the cascade when he had pulled her into his arms and she had felt his lips on hers.

"I love him!" she whispered to herself.

It was only with difficulty a little later that she roused herself on being informed that the bath was waiting for her.

A fire had been lit, and in front of it the women servants had set down a large tub and filled it with warm water.

There were two cans waiting beside it and Vesta guessed that one would contain hot, the other cold water so that it could be mixed to her liking.

She rose from the bed and took off her clothes. When the elder maid saw how creased and dusty her riding-skirt was, she said:

"I will wash and clean this for you, Gracious Lady. In fact everything you are wearing will want washing, for I hear you have come a long way."

"A very long way," Vesta answered.

It was a joy beyond words to sink into the warm water.

It was scented with flowers and the big towels with which Vesta dried herself smelt of lavender and made her think she might be back in England.

The Duchess had always insisted on her daughters cutting the lavender every year and putting it into little purple bags which they tied with purple ribbon, to distinguish them from the pink ones which held pot-pourri made from rose-leaves.

When Vesta had bathed, she explained to the younger maid that she wished to wash her hair. A basin was filled with warm water and she washed the dust from her golden head.

Then the young girl rubbed it for her in front of the fire, while the other woman disappeared, murmuring she must see about dinner.

Vesta's hair took a long time to dry, and only when it fell over her shoulders, soft and fluffy and sparkling with light, did she realise suddenly that she had nothing to wear.

The elder maid had taken away all her clothes, and

it was with a little throb of disappointment that Vesta realised that she had nothing in which she could dine with the Count.

"Will you fetch my clothes, please?" she said to the young maid.

The girl curtsied and went from the room. Vesta went on drying her hair, aware that she was beginning to feel very hungry.

The young maid came back.

"I have spoken to my mother," she said, "and she said it is impossible for the Gracious Lady to wear the dirty clothes that must be cleaned and washed. She has therefore spoken to the Honourable Bán and he suggests that you should wear these."

She held away her arms and Vesta saw that she carried two garments, the first a night-shirt made of thin white silk, the second a robe with wide sleeves not unlike those worn by monks.

She put out her hand to touch it and realised that it was of the softest white wool, a wool so fine, she guessed that it came from the very special sheep of Hungary whose wool was the rarest in the world.

"They will certainly be comfortable," Vesta smiled.

She allowed the maid to help her into the silk night-shirt which was very soft against her skin and then she slipped the white wool robe over her head.

There was a cord that she tied tightly round her small waist. She realised that the wool was so fine that large though the robe was it did not make her look fat, but clung to her body outlining the curves of her small breasts.

It was however much too long. Then to her horror she saw the maid bring a large pair of scissors and kneel down at her feet.

"You cannot cut this robe!" she cried.

"The Honourable Bán told me that I should do so," the maid answered.

"It seems almost sacrilege," Vesta thought.

But as the Count had suggested it she allowed the maid to chop away at the hem until both the night-shirt and the robe just reached the floor to cover her feet.

"I have no shoes," she now remembered and knew it

would be embarrassing to walk downstairs without them.

But at that moment the older woman came into the room. She smiled at Vesta standing in the white robe.

"I have brought you a pair of sandals, Gracious Lady," she said. "They are not very grand for I purchased them for my youngest child who is only ten. But the Gracious Lady's little feet will, I think, just fit them. They are new and have never been worn."

"How kind of you!" Vesta exclaimed. "I shall be very pleased to wear them."

The sandals were roughly made with a strap round the ankle and one to hold the toes. They were the type which had been worn by the peasants in the Mediterranean countries since the days of the Ancient Greeks.

Because they had been made for a child they fitted Vesta comfortably.

"I must do something about my hair," she said turning to the mirror on the dressing-table.

"It is not yet quite dry, Gracious Lady," the young maid replied.

It was indeed still a little damp, and when the maid brought her a piece of blue ribbon Vesta thought that she looked so strange anyway that to wear her hair loose made little difference.

So Vesta merely tied it at the nape of her neck as if she were a school girl.

She turned back the wide monk's sleeves so that they made a frame for her hands and wrists. Then feeling very shy she went from the bed-room down the staircase and into the hall.

Now she had time to look about her and to realise that the panelled walls were covered with stag's antlers of every shape and size.

There was the stuffed head of a large bear over the fireplace, and as she entered the doorway which she was certain led to the Sittingroom, she saw once again there were antlers covering the wall.

Even at a first glance it was obviously a man's room, with a huge open fireplace and a big leather-covered sofa, but she had eyes only for the Count who was standing with his back to the fire.

He too had changed his clothes, and Vesta realised it was the first time she had seen him looking elegant and dressed as a gentleman should be.

His white cravat was as high as those worn by the Dandies in London. His evening coat of blue velvet and his tight-fitting pale yellow pantaloons were both in the latest fashion.

Somehow he looked different, she thought, so different that she felt shyer, both of him and of her own appearance, than she had ever been before.

He walked across the room to meet her and taking both her hands in his raised them one after another to his lips.

"Do you feel better?" he asked.

"I feel . . . embarrassed," she answered. "It was most kind of you to send me these . . . clothes but . . ."

"You look beautiful!" he interposed. "Is that what you want me to tell you? And do you realise I have never seen your hair down before? It is very lovely."

The feeling in his voice made her blush a little as she walked towards the fireplace.

"I think," the Count went on, "that I should put you in a shrine and burn candles in front of you!"

"You are . . . making me . . . shy," Vesta protested. "I am so grateful for your thoughtfulness in lending me this beautiful robe and I much regret it has been spoilt by being cut off at the bottom."

"Unfortunately we seldom have women guests in the Hunting Lodges," the Count said. "But even if I found a Parisian couturier here, he could not have designed anything that would have suited you better."

He walked away from her to a table in the corner where he poured out a glass of wine.

"This will taste very different from what we drank last night," he said.

Vesta sipped the wine, golden and with a slight sparkle, and it made her think of the sunshine.

"It is very different," she agreed.

He was looking at her with an expression in his eyes which she half feared, but which at the same time made her thrill. And because she was nervous she looked round the room.

"It is very . . . cosy here," she said, "but very much a . . . bachelor establishment."

"Have you seen many with which to compare it?" the Count asked with a smile.

"It is what I imagine a man would choose if he arranged a house to suit his own taste," Vesta replied.

"That is true," the Count said. "I have stayed here many times, but there has never been a woman to distract my mind from the sport."

"And now I am here," Vesta said, "will you feel my . . . disturbing influence when you . . . come here . . . again."

"Are you quite certain you will not be coming with me?" the Count asked.

She turned her face away from him to look at the fire. Not for a moment could either of them forget the decision she had to make tomorrow.

It hung over them like the sword of Damocles, making her feel unsure and frightened of herself, even while it was a joy beyond words to be alone with the Count, to be able to talk to him.

"Tell me why the servants call you 'Bán'?" she asked, wishing to change the subject. "It is a word I have never heard before."

"It is Hungarian. It means a High Dignity," he answered. "Józef, that is the man's name, and his wife have worked, they tell me, in a nobleman's house before they came here. He was originally Hungarian before he came to Katōna, as are the majority of important people in the country."

"I have always longed to meet a Hungarian," Vesta said. "I have heard so much about them."

"What sort of things have you heard?" the Count asked.

"That they are very good horsemen," Vesta replied remembering what the Aide-de-camp had told her.

"And have you also been told they are good lovers?" the Count enquired.

The colour rose in her cheeks.

"There is a Hungarian song," he continued, "which says: 'our men are gallant, brave and passionate, but they can also be very tender and gentle to those they love'."

From the way he spoke, Vesta knew that he had Hungarian blood in him.

'What he has said is true,' she thought.

He was passionate and yet he could also be tender and gentle as he had been when he tied the strings of her hat under her chin and lifted her on her horse.

He had also been gentle to her last night when she had thrown herself into his arms for his protection and he had let her sleep all night against his shoulder.

The Count was watching the expression on her face.

"Am I any of those things?" he asked softly.

"All of . . . them," she answered.

She turned her face to his and once again their eyes met and they were spell-bound.

The Count rose to his feet.

"I told you not to look at me like that!" he said. "I am trying to behave as a gentleman should because you are here alone. But it is difficult, my darling, and you must not tempt me too far."

"And . . . if I . . . do?" Vesta asked in a whisper.

"Then," he answered, "I shall love you as you wish to be loved, I shall make you mine, and after that there will be no escape, now or ever."

There was a depth in his voice which told her that he was keeping himself under control with difficulty. If she drove him too hard, he would break like a dam bursting its wall and nothing she could say or do would hold him in check.

She did not look at him again, but sat staring into the fire until a door opened and Józef announced that dinner was ready.

Then the Count came to Vesta's side and held out his hand.

"We are both hungry," he said. "After dinner we will talk about ourselves, but now let us enjoy a meal that neither of us has cooked and which, if nothing else, will be edible."

"I am so hungry," Vesta answered with a smile, "that to me it will seem like the ambrosia and nectar of the gods."

"And what could be more appropriate," the Count asked, "when there is a goddess—a very alluring and adorable little goddess—to eat it with a man who is worshipping reverently at her feet?"

He slipped her arm through his and led her towards the Dining Room.

Chapter Eight

Dinner was so delicious that Vesta felt positively greedy as she ate everything she was offered.

Józef made a speech of apology as they entered the Dining Room because he said there was so little that could be provided at such short notice.

However the small golden melons were followed by trout, which Józef said had been caught after their arrival in the lake below the house.

They were not the same type of trout which the Count had snatched from the Cascade, with their pink flesh they tasted quite different, garnished with home-grown sliced almonds.

After this there were baby chickens, a whole one each, cooked with herbs and served with all sorts of delectable vegetables, some of which Vesta had never tasted before.

A kebab of baby lamb grilled on a sword was brought into the room by Józef flaming from the fire in the kitchen, and finally there were peaches, also from the garden, cooked in brandy and served with thick cream.

"I do not think I shall ever feel hungry again!" Vesta said with a smile as she finished her second helping of peaches.

"We have certainly earned everything we have eaten," the Count answered.

He sat back in the high carved chair at the top of the table as Józef brought them fruit and nuts on dishes of Sèvres porcelain.

"Do you realise, little goddess of fire," the Count

asked, "that I have never heard you call me by my name?"

Vesta smiled.

"I think I am afraid of pronouncing it wrongly—but I believe it is another form of Nicholas."

"It is," the Count agreed, "and comes from the Greek. It means—'victory for the people'."

Vesta laughed.

"It should be the name of a Revolutionary!"

"Which I am where you are concerned," he answered, "because I am determined, as you well know, to overthrow the existing order!"

She knew he referred to her position as wife of the Prince and she replied:

"I was brought up to believe that all Revolutions and all Revolutionaries are . . . bad."

"Is that what you think of me?"

She wanted to avoid the Count's eyes, but somehow he compelled her to look at him and then she was his captive, unable to look away.

"Answer me!" he commanded.

"No . . . you have been . . . all that is . . . good and kind to . . . me," she said.

As she spoke she thought how true that was! What other man could she have slept beside and been with alone, without feeling afraid or even embarrassed?

For the first time she understood that beside the dangers through which she had passed there had been other more subtle ones.

"You trust me?" he asked as if he read her thoughts.

"You know I do," she answered.

For a long moment he looked at her and she felt as if he could see deep into her heart.

"I would never harm you, my sweet life," he said slowly. "I would never do anything by thought, word or deed which would shock or frighten you."

Her eyes dropped and her eyelashes were dark against her cheeks as he went on:

"But I shall fight, contrive, coax and beguile you to give me yourself and I will never admit defeat until I am utterly and completely vanquished."

His voice seemed to echo round the room, and then

softly in a voice which charmed her heart from her
breast he said:

"Say my name! Let me hear it on your lips, so that
it will seem as soft and sweet as the kisses which at the
moment I may not give you."

"M-Miklōs," Vesta whispered and felt as if in fact
she kissed him.

Jōzef poured the Count a glass of cognac.

Vesta had sipped the sparkling white wine all
through the meal, and when Jōzef asked her if she
would have one of the sweet liqueurs that were made in
Katōna, she shook her head.

"You will enjoy it," the Count said.

"I am not used to drinking wine," Vesta replied.

"I will not allow you to drink too much," he said.

There was a caressing note in his voice which she
had noticed before when he was looking after her and
attending to her comfort.

It gave her a warm feeling of security and happiness.

At the same time she told herself that, since he was
so strong, so masterful, it was unlikely she could ever
protect him as her mother had said a woman should
protect the man she loved.

'I need him,' Vesta thought to herself, 'but how can
he possibly need me except just as someone to love?'

She suddenly felt very young and very unsophisticated.

Dressed like a man of the world, the Count seemed
somehow different from the man who had ridden
through the forest in his open-necked shirt or who with
shirt sleeves rolled up above the elbow had snatched
the trout from the Cascade.

Vesta was uncertain of herself and of him.

Here, she thought, was an older and more experienced man who was persuading her to do what she felt
in her heart was wrong.

What could she be to him in the future except a
plaything?

He was so much cleverer, so much more knowledgeable in the ways of the world, and a foreigner! Perhaps
after all he was a man she would never learn to understand even though she loved him.

"A woman should protect, sustain and inspire the man she loves."

She could hear her mother saying it, and almost despairingly Vesta thought she could do none of these things for the Count.

They stayed for some time at the table with only the candles in the silver candelabra to light the room. Then the Count rose and with his arm round Vesta's waist drew her into the Sitting-room.

The curtains had been drawn while they were at dinner, there were flames leaping above the big logs which filled the open fireplace.

There were candles, thick heavy white ones in carved stands which lit the pictures, the stag's antlers and the big bowls of fragrant flowers which stood on several side-tables.

Vesta would have sat down on the sofa, but the Count said:

"I want you to see the sunset. It can be very beautiful from the terrace. I have often watched it alone and wished there was someone with me."

"When you see something beautiful," Vesta asked, "do you always want to share it?"

"Always," he answered. "And sometimes when there is no-one the loneliness is painful."

She looked at him her eyes very wide in her small face.

"So you . . . feel like that . . . too?"

"I think we feel the same about many things," he answered.

He looked down into her eyes and she thought for a moment he was going to kiss her. Then he said abruptly as if he forced himself to move away from her:

"Come, we will go outside."

He lifted one of the heavy red velvet curtains but did not pull it back. Behind it Vesta saw the long French window that opened onto the terrace outside.

They stepped out. The terrace was flagged with square stones between which peeped tiny mauve and white flowers.

There was a profusion of bougainvilia, purple and

enchanting, climbing over the balustrade, and beside it were climbing geraniums, pink, mauve and crimson.

It was as beautiful as the sky.

The sun was sinking behind the snow-peaked mountains in a blaze of colour which faded to where overhead there was the first soft dusk of the night.

Vesta stood still just outside the window.

"It is lovely!" she exclaimed, "really lovely! I am so glad I am seeing it when I am with you."

"I think in the past," the Count said in his deep voice, "I always knew that one day I would be here at this particular moment with someone I loved. There was an emptiness in standing here alone, and yet I always came out after dinner, leaving the other men talking round the Dining-room table. But however amusing the conversation, the sunset drew me."

"And now . . . I am here with . . . you."

"I shall always remember how you look at this moment."

His dark eyes were on her face watching the sensitive curve of her lips, seeing the golden rays of the sinking sun reflected in her eyes.

For some seconds she bore his scrutiny, and then as if he compelled her against her will she turned her face and looked up at him.

"My heart, my life, my soul," the Count said very softly.

She quivered at the deep passion in his voice.

There was a sudden noise, and almost before they could turn their heads to see what it could be, a man flung his leg over the balustrade and faced them.

He was a rough, wild-looking man, with long hair and the dark eyes of a fanatic.

For a moment the Count and Vesta stared at him in astonishment. Then in a loud ugly voice he cried:

"Death to all aristocrats!" and Vesta saw that he held a pistol in his hand.

He levelled it at the Count and instinctively without thinking Vesta threw herself in front of him, her arms outstretched.

Her action took the intruder by surprise. He held his

fire for one brief second, and as he did so another shot rang out from behind him!

As the sound vibrated through the air he sprawled forward on the flag-stones of the terrace.

But as he fell he pulled his trigger!

There was a deafening report as the bullet passed through the wide sleeve of Vesta's robe and shattered the window behind her.

She stood rigid, the sound of the two shots ringing in her ears, unable to move, unable to breathe!

Then she felt the Count pick her up in his arms and carry her through the french-windows back into the Sitting-room.

She hid her face against him too shocked to realise what had happened.

He put her down very gently on the leather sofa. He looked at the hole in the sleeve of her robe and realised the bullet had not hurt her. Then without a word lifted the curtain and went back onto the terrace.

Vesta lay still where he had left her. She could hear voices now, several voices outside, though she could not understand what they were saying. It was for the moment difficult to hear anything because her ears were still ringing from the reports of the pistols.

She began to shiver and realised it was with fright. The warmth of the fire did not seem to reach her and she was very cold.

Then a wave of relief swept over her as she realised she had saved the Count's life.

Had she not thrown herself in front of him the assailant would not have hesitated before he pulled the trigger, and the shot which had come from behind him would have been too late.

She knew then that if it had been the Count who was lying dead on the terrace, she herself would have wished to die.

He was right! Love was greater and more important than anything else! Real love, the love which was irresistible and all-consuming, could not be denied.

'I will . . . stay with him because he . . . needs me,' she told herself.

She had thought that he was too powerful, too

strong, too imperious for her to be able to do anything
for him, and yet in a split second of time she had saved
him from dying.

'And, in fact for the second time!' she told herself
with a little smile, remembering how he might have
been killed by the Brigands.

'Even Mama,' she thought, 'would understand that I
am protecting the man I love when I can save his life
not once, but twice.'

She lay back against the silk cushions on the sofa,
and now she was no longer trembling and she could
feel the warmth of the fire.

The voices outside had ceased, there was only
silence. She wondered what the Count was doing and
how long it would be before he returned to her.

But even as she longed for him, the door of the Sitting-room opened and he came in.

He advanced into the centre of the room, then
stopped, looking at her. His face was very pale. Then
slowly, very slowly, as it seemed to Vesta, he came to
her side.

"How could you do such a thing?" he asked. "How
could you risk your life to save mine?"

His voice was very deep and moved with emotion.
Vesta looked up at him.

"It was . . . because I love . . . you."

For a moment he could only stare at her. Then he
said, his voice unsteady:

"Do you mean that? My precious darling, do you
mean that?"

"I mean it," Vesta whispered.

He went down on his knees and putting his arms
round her he laid his head against her breasts.

She lifted her hand a little shyly to touch his hair. It
was soft, yet firm beneath her fingers, and now with his
face hidden against her she felt a strange emotion she
had never known before.

This was her man, one who belonged to her and who
needed her love, her care and her protection.

She wanted to look after him, to keep him safe from
all harm, to sustain him. For the moment she felt almost as if he was her child rather than her lover.

Then he raised his head and asked unsteadily:

"Do you really mean, my darling, that you love me enough to give up everything else?"

"I know now I cannot . . . live without . . . you," Vesta answered.

He looked down at her.

"I swear before God, that I will devote my whole life to serving you and making you happy."

It was a vow and as his lips met hers, she knew it was a dedication and there was something spiritual in his kiss which had not been there before.

She felt an ecstasy sweep her away with all the wonder and rapture that she had known the first time he had kissed her.

Yet now they both touched the divine and there was something sacred in the wonder and glory of their closeness with each other.

The Count lifted his lips from Vesta's and she knew by the expression on his face how deeply moved he was—not only with passion but with something deeper and more tremendous, something which seemed to vibrate between them and light the whole room with a compelling radiance.

He rose from his knees and sat down beside her on the sofa. He undid the bow of blue ribbon and pulled her hair forward to bury his face in it and then kiss her again.

"I love you," he said, "I love you so overwhelmingly there are no words in which to tell you of my love."

"I love you . . . too," Vesta said. "I was thinking before you came back to me that perhaps it would be best if you went . . . alone to see the Prince to ask him to . . . release me from the marriage by proxy that took place in London."

"The Revolution is over," the Count said. "Why should you wish me to go alone?"

Vesta hesitated a moment and then as she knew he was waiting for her reply, she turned her face against his shoulder and said very softly:

"We have to face the . . . possibility that His Royal Highness may . . . refuse to do as we . . . ask."

She felt his arms tighten about her.

"And if he does?"

She knew by his sudden tenseness that he was afraid of her answer. Then Vesta said very softly:

"I will still ... come with ... you if you ... want me."

"Do you mean that?" he asked. "Do you really mean that, my beloved?"

"I mean it," Vesta answered, "because I know that without you I should be, in your own words ... 'a hollow empty shell'. I believe that God meant us for each other, and you are right, no Statesman can keep us apart."

"You would really do this for me?" the Count asked wonderingly. "You will give up everything that has been of importance to you up to now, your social position, the respect in which you believe other people hold you?"

"Nothing matters ... except you," Vesta said. "At the same time, if the Prince will not release me, then I must ... cease to ... exist."

"I do not understand."

"I mean," Vesta said in a very small voice, "that Lady Vesta Cressington-Font will have ... died on the journey from Jēno to Djilas. You will write to father and tell him I am dead, for I could not bear to hurt him as he would be hurt if he knew I was ... living with you in what to him would be ... sin."

She paused a moment and then continued bravely:

"And the people of Katōna must think I have died too. Perhaps at the hand of the Revolutionaries. The man who fired just now might have killed me."

"He could have," the Count said. "He was an Anarchist, my darling, and the soldiers have been hunting him all day."

"Then it would be easy to say that in dying he ... shot me," Vesta said. "That is, if the Prince will not ... allow me to become your ... wife."

She hesitated a moment and then she asked:

"You do ... want me as your ... wife?"

"I want you as no man ever wanted a woman before," the Count answered. "I have told you, Vesta, and I mean it, that without you I am no longer a man because you possess my brain, my body and my soul."

The deep passion in his voice made her tremble and then she cried:

"You must somehow persuade the Prince to . . . release me. Plead with him, beg him, if necessary on your knees, to let us be . . . happy . . . together."

"And if he will not," the Count said, "if we have to hide away somewhere as social outcasts, what would happen if as the years go by you grew tired of me?"

"I shall never do that," Vesta answered with a smile. "I love you, I love you so overwhelmingly that I know that my love will never change but only deepen and increase as the years go by."

She paused and then she added nervously:

"But you . . . might grow . . . tired of . . . me."

"What then?" the Count asked.

"Then as far as I was concerned, my life would be over," Vesta answered. "But it is better to love even for a short while than to exist without love . . . without happiness and without . . . you."

His lips found hers and it was impossible to speak, but only to feel . . .

It was very much later that the Count smoothed back Vesta's hair from her cheeks and kissed her eyes.

"I will tell you what I am going to do now, my darling," he said, "I am going to leave you."

"Leave . . me?"

The words were a cry.

"There are six soldiers here," he said, "who have been burying the man who tried to assassinate us. I shall take two of them with me and ride to Djilas. The other four will stay here and guard you."

"Why must you go tonight?" Vesta asked.

"For many reasons," he answered, "the first being that I must make the arrangements that you have asked of me so that we can be married as soon as possible. I cannot wait for you, Vesta, I want you now—now this very moment."

His lips found hers again. Then as he felt her stir and quiver beneath his mouth, as he saw the rise and fall of her breasts and felt her breath coming quickly from between her parted lips, he said very softly:

"I think, my sweet life, the Sleeping Beauty is at last awake."

"You have . . . awoken me," Vesta replied, "and I know now that the fire of which you spoke does . . . burn within me."

"I know that too," he answered, "and I will make it burn fiercer still until I see from the fire in your eyes that the blaze within you echoes the blaze within me."

He would have kissed her again, but then it seemed to Vesta he checked himself at the last moment.

"It is because I am afraid of that fire," he said very softly, "that I am going to Djilas tonight. I do not trust myself to stay here with you, my darling, and I think you know the reason."

Vesta gave a little laugh of sheer happiness.

"How shocked everyone would be," she said, "if they knew we were here alone and I was not yet married to you."

"I think everything we have done since we first met," the Count said with a smile, "has been unconventional and wholly unpredictable."

"That is certainly true," Vesta agreed. "Who would have imagined that having set out from England with so much pomp and circumstance, I should end up here in a bachelor Hunting Lodge, very inadequately dressed with a man I love with all my heart and soul but on whom I had never set eyes until three days ago."

The Count laughed too.

"No-one would believe it, which is perhaps a blessing."

"But it is true," Vesta said almost anxiously as if she wanted him to confirm it.

"It is true, my precious, wonderful darling," he said, "and now there is no turning back. You love me as I love you, and we shall be together for the rest of our lives."

The thought made Vesta slip her arms round his neck to pull his head down towards her.

"You will be safe?" she asked anxiously. "Promise

me you will be safe! Supposing anyone ... killed you
on the way to Djilas?"

"I shall be safe," he answered, "the soldiers tell me
that the Revolutionaries have all been rounded up.
Many had already been exiled and deported before I
came to you at Jëno. But those left were the dangerous
Anarchists, men who kill for killing's sake and not for
any particular motive."

"How did they get here in the first place?" Vesta
asked.

"They were deliberately brought into the country
from outside," the Count answered and his voice was
hard.

Vesta was sure that it was Madame Züleyha who
was responsible for their presence, and she found herself hating the unknown Turkish woman because she
might have been responsible inadvertently for the death
of the Count.

"Are you quite ... sure there are no more of ...
them?" she asked apprehensively.

"The soldiers assured me that this man was the last.
He was the most wily, the most elusive, and had already been deported from other countries for his Anarchist activities."

"And now he is dead," Vesta said with a little sigh.

"And I am alive," the Count said gently, "thanks entirely to you, my brave wonderful sweetheart."

His arms tightened about her and he said:

"I still cannot believe that you would try to save me
and risk your own life in doing so."

"It was then I knew how much I loved you," Vesta
said. "I had been worried all day trying to think what I
should decide to do, wishing there was someone who
could advise me and help me."

"I knew it was a conflict within you," the Count
said, "but it was something, my beloved, you had to
decide for yourself. I wanted to force you, you know
that. I wanted to carry you away and make you love
me, but it would not have been fair. You had to make
the choice yourself."

"No, it was made for me," Vesta contradicted. "It
was so difficult to know what was right and what was

wrong. Then when the Anarchist threatened you, I knew that you were my life."

"And now you are mine for all eternity," the Count said.

His lips were against her forehead kissing her soft skin, her little arched eyebrows and then her small straight nose.

"I want to stay here all night," he said, "I want to go on kissing you and making love to you. Very soon, Heart of my Heart, I shall kiss you from the tip of your golden head to the soles of your adorable little feet."

He kissed her small ears before he continued.

"But because I have no wish to shock you, my adorable one, I must go away. It will not be for long, I promise you that."

"I want to be your . . . wife."

"And I want to be your husband."

He kissed her again on the mouth and then as her lips clung to his, he slowly and reluctantly drew his arms from her and stood up.

"Promise me you will not leave the house until I come back for you or send a message to say that you can come to me," he said. "You can go on the terrace or walk in the garden because the soldiers will be guarding you, but do not go into the woods. I would not have a moment's peace if I thought you were in any danger."

Vesta rose from the sofa to stand beside him.

"And what shall I be feeling?" she asked, "fearing that at every inch of the way to Djilas there may be a man waiting to shoot at you, or more Brigands waiting to capture you?"

"I promise you that I will be safe," the Count answered. "I shall ride very swiftly with my escort."

Vesta hid her face against his shoulder.

"You will explain to the Prince that I meant to keep my promise I made in London, that even when you met me at Jēno I intended to come to him . . . to help him if he wanted my help?"

"I will explain exactly what has happened," the Count promised. "I can only tell the truth, Vesta, and say that I love you more than I believed it possible for any man to love any woman, and that I believe that God intended us for each other since the beginning of time."

"I am sure of that too," she said softly. "But, my darling, I am afraid ... afraid of losing you. We are too happy ... perhaps the gods will be ... jealous."

The Count laughed very softly and he lifted her face up to his.

"The gods will not be jealous of their own," he said. "You are the goddess of fire, my darling and the goddess of my heart. Because you are so perfect we shall find perfect happiness with each other."

"I hope ... that is ... true," Vesta said with a little sob.

She was afraid for him to leave her. Afraid with the new feeling that she must protect and take care of him.

He stood looking down at her in the firelight.

At her hair hanging over her shoulders, at the wide sleeves of the robe falling back from her white arms as she stretched them towards his neck, at her face soft and tender with love, her eyes very large and a little frightened.

"How can I leave you?" he asked hoarsely, "even for a moment? But once this is over we shall be together for always."

He paused a moment and then he added:

"Together day and night, my sweetheart."

"Day and ... night," she whispered.

Then he kissed her, passionately, violently, with a fierceness which told her of the pain he was suffering in leaving her, until he wrenched himself away and without looking back he walked from the room.

The door shut behind him and Vesta stood with her hands clasped forcing herself not to run after him, not to call out and tell him he must not go. But she knew the Prince must be told of what had happened.

'He will realise that there are other English girls, who will be only too pleased to come here as the reigning Princess,' she thought.

If things had gone according to plan and there had

been no Revolution, she would at this moment have been in Djilas either married or waiting to be married.

Instead now the question was would the Prince allow her to marry the man she loved, or must she go away with him into obscurity and be dead to her family and indeed to the rest of the world?

She sat down on the sofa again staring into the fire.

Even now she could hardly believe all that had happened. But she thought she had grown up in the past few days.

As the Count had said, she had been awakened by a kiss. And she was facing not the gentle romantic daydreams in which she had indulged ever since she could remember, but reality.

'Have I done the right thing?' Vesta asked herself.

She knew there was no longer any question of her not belonging to the Count as he belonged to her.

She found herself wondering where they would live. Perhaps in a small house like this!

Then with a smile she realised she had no idea whether he was rich or poor, if he was of importance in Katōna or perhaps a member of quite an obscure family.

But it did not matter.

All her life she had heard so much talk of the consequence of the Salfonts, their place in the hierarchy in the aristocracy, of the respect they commanded at Court, the manner in which they were admired by the social world.

Vesta would not have been human if she had not realised that every door in the *Beau Monde* was open to her because of her antecedents.

There was no noble family in the whole of England which would not have welcomed her as a daughter-in-law, there was no man however distinguished who would not have been proud to take her as his wife.

And now all she wanted to do was marry a man of whom she knew nothing.

He was a Count, but she was well aware this might mean very little, since foreign titles were many more in number than English ones. The sons of a Count, how-

ever many there were in the family, all took the same
rank as their father.

Perhaps he was very poor, perhaps she would no
longer be surrounded by flunkeys and servants of every
sort and description. Perhaps there would not be a profusion of horses and carriages and all else that she had
grown to expect as appertaining to the comforts of life.

'But it is not important, none of it is of the least importance,' she told herself. 'If he is very poor I will
cook for him, I will look after his house and love him.
That is all that matters.'

She wished now she had talked to him of the future.
But there had been so little time.

'Even if we have to live in a cave,' she told herself
with a smile, 'I shall be content and happy. We shall be
. . . together.'

She waited in the Sitting-room for nearly an hour.

With a new intuition that she would not have felt before, she guessed that the Count would not wish to see
her again, having once said goodbye.

He would however have to change his clothes, putting on again the riding-breeches and boots he had
worn for their journey over the mountains.

'I must give him time to go away,' she thought, 'before I retire to bed.'

She had known it was difficult for him to leave. He
had wanted to stay with her. He had wanted to go on
kissing her. They could have sat in front of the fire in
the Sitting-room until it was dawn, but he had been
right in saying he should leave when he did.

'He is always right,' Vesta told herself, 'and I will
obey him and do everything that he wishes me to do.
Always . . . because I love him.'

It seemed to her the house was very quiet and she
was certain that the Count had by now ridden away
with his escort of two soldiers.

She opened the door of the Sitting-room and went
into the hall. Józef was there waiting for her. He handed her a lighted candle. Bowing he said:

"Good night, Gracious Lady, I hope you sleep well.
God be with you."

Vesta smiled at him.

"Thank you, Jōzef."

She went slowly up the stairs, feeling the house was very quiet and empty.

When she reached her bed-room it was to find Jōzef's daughter was there waiting to help her undress.

She suddenly felt very tired and she wondered apprehensively if the Count felt as tired as she did. He was a man and was stronger than she was, but she wondered if she had kept him awake last night when she had slept against his shoulder.

She got into bed, but her thoughts were with the Count as she imagined him riding hard and fast through the woods until he reached the road she had seen winding through the valley which would eventually reach Djilas.

'Will he be thinking of me?' she asked and knew it was an absurd question.

They would each be thinking of the other every moment they were apart.

She tried to send him her love winging its way through the night, she tried to tell him as he galloped away from her how much she loved him and how she was unafraid of the future because she would be with him.

'I love you . . . I love you,' she repeated over and over again.

Finally from sheer exhaustion she fell asleep.

Chapter Nine

Because she was so tired, Vesta slept dreamlessly.

Very early, however, she awoke to stand at the window and see the pale morning sun glinting on the snowy tops of the mountains.

The song of the birds in the garden below, and the butterflies of every colour flitting from flower to flower, seemed to echo the happiness within her heart.

'I have never been so happy,' she told herself and knew it was because she loved and was loved.

It was difficult to keep her thoughts fixed on anything but the Count.

When the hands of the clock reached nine, she thought this was about the time that he would be able to have an interview with the Prince and found herself praying that everything would go the way they wished.

'Please God . . . help us . . . Please God let the Prince agree.'

She no longer felt any doubts or fears. She had made her decision, and this morning she knew that now, no question hovered at the back of her mind, nor was her conscience telling her she must do her duty to the Prince or to her country.

She was utterly and absolutely convinced that her duty now was to look after Miklōs, the man she loved, to be with him and to devote her whole life to him.

She had known last night that their kiss had a special significance, and that in it they dedicated themselves to each other.

'Whatever the difficulties and problems,' she thought

now, 'we are joined together indivisibly and nothing can separate us.'

Because Vesta realised that many hours must pass before she could hear from the Count or he could return for her, she rang the bell for her clothes.

Józef's pretty daugher brought them to her and she went downstairs for breakfast.

Fruit from the garden, honey from the beehives which Józef told her stood in the fields near the lake, fresh eggs from the small farm adjoining the Lodge, made the meal taste more appetising than any breakfast Vesta could remember.

When she had finished she asked if Józef's wife, who she learnt was called Dorottyo, would teach her to cook some of the dishes that were peculiar to Katōna.

'If we are very poor when we are married,' Vesta told herself, 'then at least I can cook Miklōs the food he likes.'

She imagined herself going into the local market to buy fresh fish for him, choose the best vegetables and the ripest fruit, deliberate over cheeses and sausages just as she knew the housewives of every European country took care over their shopping.

Dorottya was delighted at the idea of demonstrating how well she could cook. She showed Vesta first the *Psaria Plaki*, which was the dish which Vesta had found so delicious at the Inn at Jēno.

"It is what we ourselves would have eaten today, Gracious Lady," Dorottya explained.

"And I would like to eat it too," Vesta smiled.

She learnt how to make *Saltsa Augolé Mono*—the egg and lemon sauce which the Aide-de-camp had said was the national sauce of Greece.

"The Katōnians serve it with meat, fish and all their vegetable dishes," Dorottya told her.

There is nothing that makes two women more companionable than to cook together.

Soon Vesta and Dorottya were joking and laughing as they prepared a number of different dishes, and Vesta took the opportunity of having a lesson in the Katōnian language.

She had learnt by this time that there were so many

dialects that it was going to be hard for her to understand everybody.

But Dorottya and Józef were easier to follow than any of the other country people she had met such as Mr. Keupenski and the Brigands.

She wondered how many different dialects the Count could speak and if there were many people in Katōna with whom he could not converse.

'He must teach me,' she thought and thrilled at the idea of being his pupil even in a peasant dialect.

The morning passed far more quickly than she had anticipated, but every other minute her thoughts would go to the Count and she would feel a little tremor of fear that perhaps things were not going so well as they had hoped.

Supposing the Prince, insulted at being turned down and having made the preparations for their marriage, insisted she should go through with it?

If she then refused would he take his revenge? Supposing the Count was exiled from his own country, his lands confiscated, a price put on his head?

Vesta gave herself a little shake, realising that once again her imagination was running away with her. But even so the fear remained like a canker gnawing away at her happiness.

She remembered the hardness of the Count's voice when by the cascade he had spoken of the Prince's relationship with Madame Züleyha.

"The Prince is weak," he had said, "a weak man who had put his own desires and his own wishes before the needs and well-being of his country."

She could recall so vividly the contempt in his eyes as he had continued:

"He is a man who has deliberately for years ignored the wishes of his people, who shut his eyes to the fact that this woman was intriguing against the State and against himself."

'How could the Prince be so stupid?' Vesta wondered.

Yet Viscount Castlereagh had called His Royal Highness intelligent, and the Viscount, as one of the

cleverest men in England, should have been a good
judge.

But Katōna was a very small country and situated a
long way from the great powers who planned the fate
of Europe in London, Paris, Berlin and Vienna.

'Meeting a young man once or twice, or even experi-
encing what amounted to a State Visit to Katōna,'
Vesta told herself, 'gives no clue to what his own people think about him and his infatuation for the Turkish
woman.'

Then a thought struck her!

Had the Foreign Secretary and the Prime Minister of
England perhaps been well aware of the difficulties
Madame Züleyha was causing?

If so, had they deliberately sent her to Katōna to
marry the Prince believing that because she was English she might influence him to resist the intrigues
which, because they came from the Turkish source,
were fundamentally opposed to everything that was
Katōnian?

'Perhaps I have just been a pawn . . . a puppet made
use of for political reasons!' Vesta told herself.

For a moment she felt afraid, and then she remembered that the problem need no longer concern her.

The Count now stood between her and everything
that was frightening or unpleasant. His love would en-
fold and protect her, and she knew that in his arms she
felt a security she had never known before in the whole
of her life.

'I love him . . . I love him,' she whispered and
thought that she could entrust herself and all her difficulties into his hands.

It would not matter to her if they had to live in extreme poverty in some other country. Yet she would
not wish him to suffer for her sake.

Then she remembered the passion in his voice and
the light in his eyes and told herself that just as love
meant everything to her, so it must mean everything to
him.

'We are one! We think the same . . . we feel the
same!' she thought and only wished he was there to assure her that was indeed the truth.

It was just past noon and Vesta had come from the kitchen to wash and tidy herself before she sat down for the luncheon she had helped prepare, when she heard a carriage draw up outside.

She heard voices and held her breath. Could the Count have returned?

It was three hours ride to Djilas, for a man riding a well-bred horse. Was it possible for him to have seen the Prince and to have come back for her already?

It was with difficulty that she prevented herself from running into the hall. Then the door of the Sitting-room opened and Józef came in alone.

In his hand he carried a silver salver on which reposed a note.

Vesta took it from him and moved to the window to read it. For a moment when she opened it the writing seemed to swim before her eyes.

It was strong, upright and positive, as she had expected the Count's hand writing to be.

'Just as he is himself,' she whispered. Then she read:

Heart of my Heart, my Life, my Soul.

Everything is proceeding Smoothly, so I do not want You to be Worried.

The Prince desires to see You, but unfortunately it is impossible for Me to come for You as I would wish to do. So I must ask You, my Darling, to forgive me and to journey to the Palace, in the Carriage I have sent with this Letter as soon as possible.

The Revolution is over and there is great rejoicing in the City and I rejoice at the thought of seeing You.

Do not talk with anyone until you see Me and hurry my sweet, Wonderful, little Goddess, because every Second without You passes like a Century of empty Time. I am at Your Feet.

Miklós.

Vesta read it through twice before she turned to Józef who was waiting, with her eyes shining.

"I am to go to Djilas, Józef."

"I understand that the coachmen have their orders, Gracious Lady. But if you will permit the men to rest for only a short while, it would be better for them and the horses."

"Yes, of course, I understand," Vesta said, curbing an impulse to say that she must leave immediately.

"The Gracious Lady's luncheon is also ready," Józef said.

With an effort Vesta preceded him into the Dining-room where he served her the dishes she had helped Dorottya to cook.

She forced herself to eat slowly and sensibly, know-ing that she had a long journey in front of her.

But as soon as she had finished she ran upstairs to her bed-room, put on the jacket of her habit and her hat with the green ribbons.

She remembered how the last time she had worn it the Count had placed it on her head and tied the rib-bons with gentle fingers. She had been touched then by his consideration for her.

Now as she glanced at herself in the mirror she wished she had something new and more attractive in which to meet him.

Dorottya and her daughter had cleaned and pressed the green habit and washed the white muslin blouse.

But skilful though they were, they could not eradi-cate completely the stains and creases of a habit which had been slept in for two nights, and which had been worn riding over mountains and moving about in dirty caves.

Vesta thought a little wistfully of all the lovely gowns that were in her boxes at Jēno.

'I will be able to send for them,' she thought, 'and I will wear the very prettiest of them and watch for the admiration in Miklōs' eyes.'

She drew in her breath at the thought and thrilled, because she knew he would take her in his arms and kiss her.

She was ready, downstairs and waiting in the Sit-ting-room for what seemed to her like a long time, be-fore Józef came from the kitchen quarters to say that the coachmen were now ready for the return journey.

Vesta thanked Dorottya and her daughter for their kindness, and then with Józef she walked to the front door.

The closed carriage that the Count had sent for her was lightly built, and Vesta saw that it had especially large wheels for travelling swiftly over rough roads.

It was drawn by four magnificent horses which she looked at with pleasure. The two coachmen doffed their hats at the sight of her, as did the two out-riders who were also mounted on superb horseflesh.

She had known that the Count with his Hungarian blood would appreciate good horses!

'One day very soon,' she thought, 'we will ride together.'

Once she had imagined herself riding with the Prince. Now she knew nothing could be more wonderful than to ride with the Count, gallop with the wind in their faces, and explore his beautiful country.

She turned to thank Józef for all he had done for her and wished she had some money to give him. But he did not seem to expect it and bowed low as the footman helped Vesta into the carriage and the cavalcade set off.

As they reached the end of the drive they were joined by the four soldiers on horse-back who had been guarding the house all night.

The soldiers rode in the rear and were wise enough to avoid the dust from the carriage by keeping on the grass verges which bordered the narrow track.

Vesta thought uneasily that the Count was taking every possible precaution against her being ambushed or shot at. Then she knew he would not have said that the Revolution was over unless that were true, and there was no reason for her to be afraid.

They travelled downhill for some way, passing the lake where the trout they had eaten the night before had been caught. It was shining in the sunlight and a gaggle of wild geese rose into the air at their approach.

After several miles of winding between high fir trees, they joined another wider road.

Vesta was sure this was the one she would originally

have taken from Jēno had she been met as she had expected by Baron Milovan and the welcoming party.

Now the carriage which had been moving fairly slowly along what was little more than a track by the Hunting Lodge, proceeded at a pace which Vesta knew would have been watched admiringly in England.

At the same time, like the Count, she felt every second was slow and long drawn out because they were not together.

She sat forward to look out of the windows.

'This is his country,' she told herself. 'This is where Miklō belongs and I must love it and understand its people for his sake.'

There were small white houses with red roofs. There were farms, many of them picturesquely fashioned of wood and situated among lush fields of corn or verdant grass where fat cattle were grazing.

Above the valley on either side loomed the mountains, their sides covered thickly with trees.

'It is all so beautiful!' Vesta told herself. 'How could people not be happy in a country like this? Why should they want Revolutions, how can they wish to rebel against anything or anybody?'

Again she asked herself how the Prince could have allowed Madame Züleyha to endanger the peace and prosperity of this lovely country?

Despite her interest in seeing the countryside, her impatience to see the Count again made the hours pass slowly.

And despite her resolution not to worry but to trust him to do what was best for both of them, she could not help, as they neared Djilas, feeling apprehensive.

It was quite a large city, exquisitely situated on a broad silver river in a wide and fertile valley flanked by mountains.

Vesta saw it at a distance from higher ground, and it was somehow as she had expected it to look with its spires and high steeples, its towers and red-roofed houses.

The valley through which she had been passing had been mainly green except for colourful flowers growing on either side of the road. But now as they came into the outskirts of the town she saw, just as she had done in Jeno, that there were flowers everywhere.

In the orange and lemon groves which grew just outside the city there were flowers of every size and colour, the houses were decorated with bougainvillia and clematis growing up the walls, and the balconies were filled with variegated blossoms.

The people too, Vesta noticed, had hung out flags from their windows, and she knew that this was part of the rejoicing of which the Count had spoken because the Revolution was over.

'Now they will have peace,' Vesta told herself.

She wondered if the Prince would soon find a wife to reign with him, who would work for his people and try to understand them.

Just for a moment she had the uncomfortable feeling that it should have been her task. Perhaps in refusing to marry the Prince she was forcing him back into the arms of Madame Züleyha or someone like her.

Then she told herself the Prince had no personal need of her help while the Count, she was convinced, could not do without her.

'That is what all women desire,' she thought. 'To be wanted, to know one is indispensable.'

Looking out of the window she realised the carriage was not taking her in through the centre of the city but along quiet side streets where there were few people about.

Perhaps after all, she thought, the Prince had refused to release her from their legal marriage and she would, therefore, have to go away secretly into obscurity with the Count.

'It does not matter so long as he loves me,' she told herself re-assuringly.

She had the impression, although she was not certain where she had learnt it, that the Palace was in the very centre of Djilas.

She was sure of this when having travelled some way along the river they seemed to turn almost in a circle, still keeping to the side-streets but now obviously moving towards the middle of the city.

Then she saw a high brick wall, and having driven

beside this for a short distance they came to an entrance with gates carrying the Royal Coat-of-Arms but
which was manned only by two soldiers.

The gates were opened for the carriage and now
Vesta saw green lawns, sparkling fountains and a profusion of flowers.

It was only a quick glimpse, for they were driving
along what she was sure was a back drive, flanked with
flowering trees.

The carriage drew up at what was obviously a side-
door of the Palace.

A footman resplendent in gold lace opened the carriage door, and Vesta stepped out looking anxiously
into the doorway ahead because she hoped she might
see the Count waiting for her.

There was however only a Major-domo who present-
ed her with a note on a silver salver.

The hall into which she had walked was small and
not very impressive. She took the note and turning to
the light of the window read it quickly.

> You are here, my Beloved, and I am waiting to
> see You more Impatiently than I have ever waited in
> my whole Life. But because you are a woman, and
> the most beautiful and adorable woman in the
> World, I know You will wish to wash and change
> before We meet. Hurry, my Precious One, because I
> need You so Desperately. I am waiting and My arms
> are aching for You.
>
> Miklōs.

Vesta closed the letter and resisted an impulse to kiss
it. Only the Count, she thought, could be so consider-
ate, so understanding!

It was as if their minds worked in unison, so that he
knew that she longed to look her best for him, to dis-
card her travel-stained clothes and change into something in which he would admire her.

It was true also that the journey had been dusty.

There could not have been any rain in Katōna for
some time and when the carriage windows were open